Mort Ziff
Is Not Dead

CARY FAGAN

Mort Ziff
Is Not Dead

CARY FAGAN

PUFFIN

an imprint of Penguin Random House Canada Young Readers,
a Penguin Random House Company

Published in hardcover by Puffin Canada, 2017

Published in this edition, 2018

ScoutAutomatedPrintCode

Manufactured in the U.S.A.
2nd Printing
Library and Archives Canada Cataloguing in Publication

Fagan, Cary, author
Mort Ziff is not dead / Cary Fagan.

Previously published: 2017.
ISBN 978-0-7352-6629-2 (special markets)

I. Title.

PS8561.A375M67 2018   jC813'.54   C2018-900328-6

Library of Congress Control Number: 2016948507

Cover design by Lisa Jager
Cover art by (Flamingo) © Bluedarkat/Shutterstock.com;
(hat) © dragance 137/istockphoto.com; (billboard) © miloart/istockphoto.com

www.penguinrandomhouse.ca

Penguin
Random House
PUFFIN CANADA

For my father, Maurice Fagan,
with much love

Counting Doozy Dots

My brothers were only one and two years old when I was born, but even so, it was as if they got together and decided that three was a crowd. Who needs another brother? At least that's how it felt, because I never really fit in with them. And they never made it easy for me.

For example, it was always a mistake to compete with them. If I got suckered into having a bicycle race, Marcus (the older one) would secretly let half the air out of my tires. If I agreed to a match of miniature golf, Larry (the middle one) would bump my arm while I was putting. If I refused to play cards or Monopoly, the two of them would beg me on their hands and knees, promising not to cheat. Then, of course, they did. Making me lose was to them the funniest thing in the world. They never got tired of it.

Which was one reason it was so fantastic that I won the "Guess the Doozy Dots" contest at Shoppe Heaven Mall.

Doozy Dots were these little candies with funny faces on them that fizz and pop in your mouth. At the mall there was a special promotion. Women in green elf outfits were standing around a giant glass jar of Doozy Dots. It must have been ten or twenty feet high. You had to guess how many candies were in the giant jar.

This happened on the last Saturday in October, a super-beautiful day, maybe one of the last nice days before winter. I wanted to be outside, flying the balsa-wood airplane that I had just finished building. It had a rubber-band motor and a plastic propeller, and I couldn't wait to try it. But my parents thought that this was the perfect day for me and my brothers to buy new shoes. Not running shoes even, but ugly leather shoes that had, in my mother's immortal words, "healthy arch support."

So there we were, pushing our way through the crowds to where the green elf women were handing out forms and little pencils. On the form, you were supposed to write down your guess, along with your name and address.

"I'm going to win this for sure," Marcus said, holding the paper against a post and squinting as he filled it in.

"Don't get too excited, Marcus," Dad said. "Nobody wins these things."

"Well, I am. I'm picking my number right now. I'm going to guess ten billion and eight."

"That might be a little high," Mom said.

"No, it isn't. It's exactly right. I calculated." He tapped the side of his head with the little pencil.

"How did you calculate it?" Larry asked. He hadn't filled out his form yet. He always thought Marcus was right. He thought Marcus was a genius.

"You think I'd tell you, flea-brain?"

"Okay then," Larry said. "I'm going to put down the same number. Ten billion and eight."

"You can't do that! Mom, Dad, tell Larry he can't."

"Never mind," Larry sang, printing carefully. "I'll put down ten billion and *nine*."

Marcus began to chase Larry, but Larry managed to stuff his form into the slot in the plastic container made to look like a box of Doozy Dots. I filled out my own form. I put down a smaller number. I put down 4,243. I didn't calculate at all. I just pulled it out of the air.

When Marcus gave up trying to catch Larry, he came over to look at my form. "Are you kidding me?" he said, and proceeded to laugh his head off. Actually, I wish he had really laughed his head off so that it rolled all the way down the length of the Shoppe Heaven Mall.

I put my form into the box and we all went to the shoe store. Marcus and Larry begged for loafers but Mom insisted we get three identical pairs of lace-up shoes. My brothers immediately began to scuff them up on the way back to the car. We drove our creaky old Buick home, by which time I had to start my chores and couldn't fly my balsa-wood airplane.

All of us forgot about the Doozy Dots contest. We forgot about it for a whole month.

Blue Chip

"Hey, Wormy, there's a letter for you. Maybe it's from some *girrrl* . . ."

It's a Jewish tradition to name kids after a dead relative, and I was named Norman—Norman Fishbein—after my great-grandfather Nachman. All I knew about Nachman was that he had seven children and a long beard, and when he wasn't hunched over a cobbler's bench making shoes, he was at the prayer house.

But I lived in the new world, in Toronto, Canada. And it was the year 1965, the modern age. We had telephones and televisions (color!) and transistor radios. An astronaut named John Glenn had gone around the earth in a space capsule. Our own prime minister, Lester Pearson, had won the Nobel Peace Prize. My dad wished that he could drive a Mustang convertible, and my mom thought that we should start eating some new health food called yogurt, which came from Sweden or some place like that.

All of this is why my name was Norman. My parents sometimes called me Normy, which was okay as long as nobody from school was around. But I hated the nickname that my brothers called me. *Wormy.*

We were hanging around the living room when Marcus came in, Mom and Dad reading the newspaper on the sofa and Larry and I in the comfy armchairs. "A letter?" said Larry, looking up at Marcus, who was holding an envelope in his hand. "Who'd be writing to you, Wormy? Maybe it's a new pen pal. Maybe it's some kid in Iceland or Borneo who smells just as bad as you."

"I still think it's a girl," Marcus said, waving the envelope around. "Some girlfriend with the cooties who wants to *smooch* with you."

"I don't have a girlfriend or a pen pal," I grouched. The only letters I got were from the Boy Scouts, asking me if I wanted to rejoin. I had lasted in the Boy Scouts exactly two weeks.

"Come on, boys," Dad said without looking up from the newspaper. "Give Norman his letter."

But Marcus didn't give it to me. He took a step forward and peered at it, straightening a pair of imaginary glasses. "Let me see. It's from Blue Chip Promotions. Tell us, Wormy, do you know anybody named Chip?"

Larry got up and snatched it from Marcus's hand. "I think it's a parking ticket. Tell us, Wormy, did you leave your tricycle near a fire hydrant?"

This whole time I just sat in the armchair, not even trying to get it. I'd had long experience with my brothers holding back something that was mine. I just had to wait for the right moment, which was right . . . now! I lunged forward, stretching over the coffee table to grab the letter.

I also knocked over Mom's mug of tea.

A lot of shouting and finger-pointing followed, but my parents tried not to pick sides. They said we were all at fault, even as the three of us wiped up the spill with some rags that I got from the kitchen.

Of course, Marcus and Larry shoved each other the whole time.

At last, peace returned, more or less, and I returned to the armchair. I used a butter knife to slice open the envelope and then pulled out the letter. Silently I read it to myself.

Blue Chip Promotions
136 Brockton Street, Suite 1120
Ottawa, Ontario

November 27, 1965

Dear Mr. Fishbein,

Congratulations! Your guess
of 4,243 Doozy Dots for our
promotional contest was correct!
You may be interested to know that
you are the only person ever to guess
the exact number!

Thank you for participating in
another Blue Chip promotion!
We hope that you will continue to
enjoy the flavor–bursting fun of
Doozy Dots!

Yours truly!

Geoffrey Klinker,
Vice-President

My first thought was that Geoffrey Klinker sure did like using exclamation marks. My second thought was: I won?

I said it out loud.

"What's that?" Dad asked. "You're whispering, Norman."

"I said that I won."

"That's nice," Mom said. "What did you win, sweetheart?"

"The Doozy Dots contest. The one in the mall, remember?"

Everything stopped. Everyone looked at me. "No way," Marcus said. "With that lame guess?"

"What did you win?" Larry asked. "A stupid baseball hat? A pencil case?"

"Well done, Normy," Dad said. "What did you actually win? If it's a carton of candies, you can't eat them all at once. They'll make you sick."

I didn't know what I had won. I looked again at the letter but it didn't say. And then I noticed something else in the envelope, a slip of paper. It was a check. I knew what a check looked like because every year on my birthday I got one for five dollars from Uncle Shlomo. But this one wasn't for five dollars.

I tried to speak.

"Norman?" said my mother.

"I won . . . I won . . . a thousand dollars."

Silence. Marcus and Larry had their mouths open. My parents both looked as if I'd just told them that I had been selected for the next space launch.

I put the check back in the envelope. "I guess I'm rich," I said.

Vault

Everybody wanted to look at the check. Marcus and Larry even argued over it, grabbing the check from each other until they tore the corner. I got so upset that I used a word not allowed in our house, but my parents were just as mad at them and didn't notice.

Dad got the Scotch tape and fixed the corner, assuring me that it was still good. But I knew that check wouldn't be safe until I put it in the bank. Dad said the bank was closing in half an hour but

I insisted. So the five of us drove in the clanking Buick to the stone building with big pillars on either side of the doors. We waited in line, Mom and Dad and Marcus and Larry behind me, until finally it was my turn.

The bank teller was a man with a little mustache. "May I help you?" he said.

I slid my bankbook across the marble counter. "Can you tell me how much money I have in my account?" I asked.

"Of course. As it says in your book, you have seven dollars in your account."

I slid the check toward him. "I wish to make a deposit."

"Very good." The bank teller got a slip of paper and began to fill it in. He asked me to sign the paper and then he stamped it. He put my account book into a machine that began to bang away like a typewriter. He took it out again. He put the slip of paper and the check in a drawer under the counter.

"That's it?" I asked.

"Yes, sir."

"Can you tell me how much I have in my account now?"

The teller looked at me. Then he opened my account book. "You now have one thousand and seven dollars in your account."

"That's right," I said. "Would you please put the check into the vault?"

"I assure you, that check is perfectly safe."

"But if a bank robber came—"

"Please, sir," he interrupted. "We prefer not to mention such things out loud."

"I'd really be happier if you put it in the vault."

"I'll have to get the manager."

"I don't mind waiting."

By now there was a considerable line of people behind me, all trying to do their banking before closing. But I didn't move from my spot. The teller took the check and walked over to a man who must have been the manager, and the two whispered with their heads close together. The teller pointed to me. The manager frowned. At last the manager went over to the enormous steel door of the vault, dialed the combination, put in a large key that he kept on a chain and opened the big door. It must have been three feet thick. The two of them walked into the vault and disappeared. A moment later they came out again and the manager shut the enormous door.

The teller returned. "It is now in the vault. I hope, sir, that you are satisfied."

"Perfectly satisfied," I said.

We got into the car and drove home again.

Ha, Ha, Ha

"I think," Mom said, "we shouldn't talk about that money for a while."

No doubt she was responding to my brothers, who kept whining about how it wasn't fair and that I should be splitting the money with them. I was afraid that my parents might agree, but instead they insisted that Marcus and Larry just stop. "Norman won it," Dad pronounced. "Simple as that. It's his money."

Not talking about it didn't mean that nobody thought about it. My brothers were so resentful that for the next two days they were extra mean to me, running ahead so that I had to trudge to school on my own, never passing to me during ball-hockey games in the driveway. At the dinner table, whenever I said something Marcus would say, "Did you hear a noise?" and Larry would answer, "It must be a fly buzzing around."

Fine, I thought, I didn't need them either. That weekend I took my balsa-wood airplane to the park so that I could fly it at last. It was cold—Dad had said that he could smell an early snow coming. A wind was blowing, never good for flying, but if it did snow, then I wouldn't be able to try again until the spring. Carefully I turned the propeller, winding the heavy rubber band inside the fuselage. I cocked back my arm and launched it upward. The propeller whirred, pulling the plane higher, over the teeter-totter and the swings, high into the cloudy sky.

"Yahoo!" I cried, running behind as the plane veered to the right and began to circle up. A gust of wind from behind pushed it higher until it was almost vertical, and then it tipped downward. It took a moment for me to realize the plane was heading right toward me. I covered my head with my arms and ran.

Crack! The plane missed me by a couple of feet, smacking the hard ground. Picking it up, I saw that the nose was pushed in and the struts of one wing had shattered like the thin bones of a bird.

"Another disaster," I said out loud. Then I put it on my shoulder and carried it home. In the house, I put the broken plane in the closet beside my three other wrecked planes. Outside my window a few large flakes of snow came down. I wondered what some of my friends from school were doing. Like Daniel Tamber, whose dad was a dentist and made a lot more money than my parents. Daniel went to tennis camp every summer and had even been to France. Or Jessica Garwin. Jessica's parents were land developers, whatever that meant. She took horseback riding lessons and said that when she turned sixteen she was going to get her own horse. My dad was a plumber and general repairman and my mom worked part-time doing the accounting for her sister's dress shop. Dad could have gone to college but he preferred to work with his hands and went to vocational school instead. He said he was like a doctor, except that instead of working on people he operated on toilets and put bandages on walls.

All of this thinking about my parents brought me back to the thousand dollars. For us, it was a lot of money. I worried that my parents would want me to use it for something practical, like putting a new roof on the house or buying a car that didn't break down all the time. Or maybe they would want me to put it in the bank to pay for college so that I could become an engineer and design airplanes, like I always talked about. Sure, the money was in my bank account now, but that didn't mean it was really mine.

Someone knocked on my door. I knew it wasn't Marcus and Larry because they never knocked. They just barged in, throwing grapes at me, or aiming squirt guns, or trying to force me to put on a pair of my mom's nylons. It had to be my parents.

"Enter laughing," I said. That was what I always said when my parents knocked on my door. I think it's the name of a play or movie or something, but it's just one of the things I say and my parents always come in pretending to laugh. Pretty lame, but we do it anyway.

My parents came in but they didn't pretend to laugh. They closed the door and sat on the end of my bed. They had the same serious expressions as the time they told me that we couldn't have a dog because my father was allergic.

"Norman," Dad said.

"Uh-huh?"

"About the money you won. We think it's time to talk about it."

"Okay."

Mom said, "We've decided that we want you alone to choose what to do with the money."

I sat up. "Can you say that again?"

"You heard your mother right, kiddo."

"You mean it? I can really decide? Anything I want?"

"That's right." Dad nodded. "And we want you to choose because we know what a smart and level-headed boy you are. Sometimes I think your older brothers could learn a thing or two from you. If they won the money, they'd probably want to spend it on toys or bikes or who knows what. But you wouldn't."

"I wouldn't?"

"Not a responsible boy like you. Your brothers aren't even aware that the house needs a new roof. Or that the car is fifteen years old."

"Oh."

"And of course there's your college fund," Mom said. "That would be a very good place to put any that's left over. Education is just so important." She and Dad got up from the bed. "But it's your decision, Norman. And you take your time. There's no rush."

My parents both smiled at me and then left the room, closing the door behind them. But a second later they opened the door again.

"We forgot," Dad said. The two of them pretended to laugh.

"Ha, ha," I said back. They closed the door again. "Ha, ha, ha," I said to nobody, collapsing onto my bed.

Funny Haircuts

I spent the next week torturing myself about what to do with the money. I couldn't stop thinking about it. My thoughts buzzed and hummed like a swarm of bees around my head.

In school I couldn't concentrate at all. Inside my history book I snuck the latest catalogue from the Blisto Balsa-Wood Airplane Company, thirty-four pages of amazing kits. I skipped over the advanced kits that until now I had just dreamed about and looked only at the "professional level" kits. The one I liked the best was a 1915 Bristol Scout biplane with a six-foot wingspan, working gas engine and a remote control so that you could make it dive and do figure eights and come down for a perfect landing. Man, was it a beauty. I figured it would take me five or six months to build. It was way too big to fly in the backyard or even the neighborhood park; I'd have to get Dad to drive me out to some farmer's field. The price was $253.

But that was less than a third of the money I had won. I had a lot of ideas for spending the rest. Not long ago I'd seen a full drum kit in the shop window of a music store. (I could learn to play, couldn't I?) Or if I got an Italian racing bike, I'd be able to speed past my brothers for the first time. Or how about a telescope or an ice cream maker for my room?

It seemed weird to me that with this momentous decision hanging over my head I still had to go to school and do my homework, dry the dishes and take out the garbage. And it seemed just as strange that everybody else was going about their regular routines too. After school, Marcus would go down in the basement and practice his Ping-Pong serves. Marcus was crazy about Ping-Pong. He had saved up for his own top-of-the-line racquet, the Quest 2000, and wouldn't let me or Larry use it. He had found a book on Ping-Pong in the school library and he took it out once a month to read, over and over again. He invited all the kids on our street to come over and play just so that he could demolish them. Even his backhand was killer. And when there were no kids around, and Larry and I were tired of being beat twenty-one to nothing, he would stay down by himself and practice his serves.

While Marcus went down to the basement after school, Larry would head for the living room. Then he would turn on the television, sit on the broadloom about three feet from the screen and watch Planet Furball.

Is there anybody who doesn't know what Planet Furball is? Maybe if they're living on a desert island. Planet Furball is this TV show about a planet ruled by talking cats. A long time ago there was a war that poisoned the planet's air and water, so the cats have to live inside this giant dome. To keep the dome operating, the cats need the help of these super-intelligent rats who are the only other surviving animals and understand stuff like science and engineering. The rats have agreed—on the condition that the cats stop eating meat. The cats have to go along with it, but they aren't too happy about being vegetarian. So the two species have this uneasy truce, but they don't trust each other. You can see pretty easily what sort of conflicts might happen.

Personally, I thought the show was dumb. But Larry, he watched every new episode after school and reruns on the weekend. He read *Planet Furball* comic books. He belonged to the *Planet Furball* Fan Club. He even kept a notebook with a page for every character, every episode, and drawings of how the dome worked, farming, costumes, everything. I wasn't sure if Larry would rather have been a cat or a rat, but I'm absolutely certain that if he could he would have chosen to live on that polluted planet.

One afternoon when Marcus was down in the basement whacking Ping-Pong balls and Larry was lying in front of the TV soaking up *Planet Furball*, my mother asked me to help her unpack groceries in the kitchen. A Beatles song came on the radio and she started singing along, with a lot of "love you's" and "yeah, yeah, yeah's."

Mom really liked the Beatles; in fact, she had cut a picture of them out of the newspaper a year ago and it was still on the fridge. I put a carton of milk in the fridge, closed the door and looked at the grainy picture again. It showed them splashing and goofing around in the ocean. The words underneath said that the Beatles had come to Miami Beach for their second appearance on *The Ed Sullivan Show* and that they had liked the place so much they decided to stay a week.

I couldn't tell which Beatle was which. To me they looked like four funny haircuts. I knew that Miami Beach was in Florida. I had never seen the ocean. The only beach I had ever been on was all stones, on a lake that was ice-cold and slimy on the bottom. I'd never seen a palm tree. Those Beatles sure looked like they were having a great time. They looked like they were in paradise.

And then I knew.

I really did. I knew the perfect thing to do with the money. I just didn't know if my parents would agree with me.

My Big Announcement

After school on Thursday, Marcus had his bar mitzvah lesson. He was the first of us to be having his bar mitzvah, and at first Marcus was excited because he was going to "become a man." But then he found out how much work it was. Naturally, Larry and I, who would be up next, were curious to see what it was about.

Having a bar mitzvah lesson meant watching Mr. Grossman drive slowly up in his car and park it with two wheels up on the curb. It meant listening to Mr. Grossman sigh heavily as he sat down at the dining room table and opened the Hebrew book. It meant not only reading Hebrew aloud, but also singing the words to the proper melody. It meant answering Mr. Grossman's questions, questions that went like this: "Yes, you know the words. But the meaning! Do you know what the words mean, Marcus? Do you understand how deep they are? Do you see the moral implications?"

Standing outside the doorway, Larry and I would look at each other and gulp. Becoming a man wasn't going to be easy.

At last, Mr. Grossman finished the lesson. As always, he patted Marcus on the head and said, "You're a good boy, a smart boy, but you don't study hard enough." Then he gave Marcus a hard lemon candy, went out the door and pulled his car—bump, bump—off the curb to drive slowly away.

We sat down for supper. Marcus, who was always hungry after his lesson, picked up the plate of chicken. But Larry leaned halfway over the table and speared a chicken leg with his fork. "Thanks, big brother. Mighty kind of you."

"Yeah, and I hope it tastes like dog poop."

"There's no need to make a big stink about it."

"That's enough, you two," Dad said. "You're going to spoil our appetites. Let's have a civilized meal with interesting conversation for once. I'll start. Today I had this fascinating work problem. You see, whoever put in the original pipes—"

"Dad, you said interesting," Marcus groaned. "Like if the pipe turned out to be full of radioactive snakes."

"And you had to fight them off with a wrench," Larry added. "But one of them bit your nose off."

"All right, boys," Mom said, passing the beans. "There's such a thing as having too much imagination. What about you, Norman? Do you have anything interesting to tell us?"

"I guess so," I said, suddenly nervous. "I've decided what to do with the money I won."

"Let me guess," Larry said resentfully. "You're going to buy elevator shoes with real elevators in them."

"I know," Marcus said. "You're going to hire a movie star to be your friend. She'll follow you around saying, 'You're so smart, Norman. You're so handsome, Norman.'"

"Ignore your dear brothers," Mom said. "Tell us all what you're going to do with the money."

She and Dad smiled at each other. I knew what they were thinking: *Is it a new roof or a new car?* I looked down at my lap and said, "I want us all to go to Miami Beach. At Christmas."

"What?" said Dad.

"Miami Beach!"

Marcus and Larry jumped out of their chairs. They began dancing around the table, singing, "We're going to Miami Beach, we're going to Miami Beach . . ."

"Shush, you two," Mom scolded. "Sit down and eat your dinner. Norman, this is a very big surprise. Can you tell us why?"

"It's just that we hardly ever go anywhere. And when we do, we always drive to some campground and then sleep in a tent. I want to stay in a nice hotel. And see the ocean. It's not just for me—everybody would enjoy it. Couldn't we all use a real holiday? I know it's good to be practical. But once in a while you have to have fun too."

For once my brothers didn't speak. It was like they were holding their breath, waiting for my parents to decide.

"It's very thoughtful of you to think of us all," Mom said. "A real vacation would be nice, don't you think, Phil?"

"It's always good to do something together as a family," Dad answered.

"You mean we can go?" I asked.

Dad ruffled my hair. "If your mother agrees, then I do too."

"I guess we're going to Miami Beach," Mom said.

"Okay!" I said, grinning. Marcus and Larry jumped out of their chairs again.

"Now listen, you two," Mom said. "Thank Norman for wanting to share his good fortune with all of us."

Marcus came over to me. He put a hand on my shoulder. Then he smacked the side of my head. "Thanks a lot, dumb-bum!"

"Yeah, thanks gizwack!" Larry pulled my ear.

They ran out of the kitchen screaming at the top of their lungs, their hands waving in the air.

Dad rolled his eyes. "I don't suppose we could leave them at home."

The Sky-High Travel Agency

Now that the decision was made to go to Miami Beach, I started to worry. Since the holiday was my decision, I figured that it was up to me to make all the arrangements. For two nights I lay in bed wondering how an eleven-year-old could buy plane tickets and find a hotel. Finally, I decided to ask my dad for advice.

I could tell he was trying not to laugh. "Really, Norm," he said, ruffling my hair. "You're a kid, remember? You're not supposed to know how to do these things."

I wasn't? That was a big relief to me. "We'll go to a travel agency," he said. "After all, they're the experts."

So Dad and I drove downtown. The first thin layer of snow had quickly melted, but the sky was gray and it was cold. Dad parked in front of a window filled with posters for England, Sweden, Mexico, Australia. I'd never thought much about traveling before—I'd never even been on an airplane. But suddenly the possibility of seeing the world opened up before me.

I had this idea that the Sky-High Travel Agency would look glamorous inside, but instead I saw a dented metal desk, a flickering fluorescent light overhead and a tired-looking woman eating french fries from a paper bag as she spoke into the telephone.

"I'm sorry but there's really nothing that I can do about a hurricane. You're just going to have to go somewhere else. Why don't you think about it and call me back."

She hung up and gave us what my dad always called a "professional" smile. "May I help you?" she asked.

Dad gave me a nod. So I said, "We want to go to

Miami Beach. At Christmas. Me and my parents and my two brothers."

"A very popular choice. That is high tourist season, of course, so it's more expensive."

"I have the money. It's in a bank vault."

"How interesting. Well, I can put you on an Air Canada flight directly to Miami. That's a hundred and twenty dollars return for each person. What about accommodation? There are some decent motels about an hour from the beach."

"No. We want to be right on the beach. And not in a motel. We want a nice hotel. A really nice hotel."

"In that case, I recommend the Royal Palm Hotel."

"I've heard of it," Dad said. "The Royal Palm Hotel is owned by that millionaire, Herbert Spitzer."

"That's right; he lives on the top floor. They say he keeps a refrigerator full of money. And that he wears a suit made out of gold. It's a beautiful place, made of real coral from the sea, and it's first-class. The restaurant is divine and the beach is gorgeous. Take a look."

Behind her was a wobbly bookshelf heaped with brochures. She searched through them and came up with one that she put on the desk. It had a picture of the hotel on the front. I'd never seen anything so beautiful in my life. It looked like a pink castle. Inside were pictures of the marble lobby, the outdoor swimming pool and the pale sand of the beach against the blue ocean.

"How much does it cost?" Dad asked.

"You would need a two-room suite. That's seventy-five dollars a night."

I asked her if I could borrow a pencil and a piece of paper. Five airplane rides would cost $600. Six nights in the hotel added up to $450. That made a total of $1,050.

"Dad," I said, "could you lend me fifty dollars?"

"I think I can donate that amount."

I smiled. "That's where we want to stay," I said. "The Royal Palm Hotel."

"You couldn't have made a better choice," the woman said, just as the telephone started to ring. She sighed. "I don't suppose that you would take me with you."

How could I possibly wait two and a half weeks before our holiday started? It snowed and then snowed again and every day the temperature dropped. Across the road, I watched two little kids build a snowman with a carrot nose.

"This trip is going to be amazing," Marcus said. "I'm going to swim to the bottom of the ocean and find a shipwreck. I'm going to bring up a gold sword."

"I'm going to find one too," Larry said. "And mine will have diamonds and rubies on it."

"Yeah, but mine will be really *sharp*."

"Nobody is playing with swords," Dad said.

Mom went outside to clear snow off the car. Then we drove to the mall to buy new bathing suits. I was worried that the cost of the bathing suits would come out of the thousand dollars, but Mom said that she and Dad would pay for all the extras, including our meals.

First we went to the boys' department, where my brothers and I got identical blue and white striped bathing suits. Dad got a green one. Then we had to go to the women's department. Mom made Marcus and Larry swear they wouldn't pretend to talk to the mannequins or make fun of the women's brassieres.

She went into the dressing room, and when she came out again Dad said, "If it isn't Miss Canada 1965. You look great, honey." But Marcus, Larry and I stared in horror. Our mother in a *bikini*!

"Mom, you can't!" Marcus pleaded.

"Don't be mean, sweetheart."

"But he's right," Larry said. "You're our mom. You're old."

"I'm thirty-seven. That isn't old. Norman, what do you think?"

The truth was that I felt the same way as my brothers. Moms shouldn't wear bikinis. But I didn't want to hurt her feelings.

"I think it looks nice, Mom."

Marcus sidled up to me. "Sleep lightly tonight, brother," he whispered. "Because you're going to pay for this."

As if he had to tell me.

The snowplow pushed itself down the street, forming tall banks along either side. Kids built forts and threw snowballs at one another, shouting into the frosty air. Any other winter I would have been out there too, but all I could think about as I looked out the fogged-up window was Miami Beach.

Walking to school, I kept my scarf over my mouth and nose but still the wind hurt my face. My eyes teared up. Dad got our beat-up suitcases out of the basement. He went to a used bookstore downtown and bought himself a paperback copy of a fat novel called Exodus to read on the beach. Larry lay under his desk lamp with his shirt off, saying that he was getting a head start on his tan. Marcus began doing push-ups because he wanted to look like a lifeguard. Larry laughed. "They'll take one look at you and decide they'd rather go under."

At last Friday arrived, the last day of school. Our flight was the next day. Our suitcases were packed and waiting at the door. Dad had to go on an emergency job to deal with a frozen pipe. Trying to come home again, his car wouldn't start and he had to get it towed. He walked in with ice in his hair. "It's like Siberia out there," he said.

Mom sent us to bed early. I lay in the dark, too excited to sleep. When I went to the bathroom I heard my parents talking in their room. They said that if the weather was bad the airplane might not be able to take off.

In bed, I worried until at last I fell asleep. In the morning, Marcus and Larry woke me up. They didn't dump cold water on my face or try to scare me. They just nudged me gently.

"Norman," Marcus said. "It doesn't look good."

I hurried out of bed and ran to the front window. Everything was white. The street had disappeared.

"Go ahead and cry if you want to, Normy," said Larry. "I wouldn't blame you."

I heard Dad's voice. "Why are you kids just standing around? Get dressed!"

We turned around. Dad wore a baseball cap and sunglasses. "Do you really think we can go?" I asked. "Will the plane be able to take off?"

"We won't know until we get there. And getting there is the first thing we have to do. My car won't get through, but if there's anyone who can get us to the airport, I know who it is."

"Uncle Shlomo!" cried Marcus.

Dad nodded. "He's on his way."

The Runway

Uncle Shlomo was actually my dad's uncle, which made him our great-uncle. He had a heavy Yiddish accent, a bald head and a barrel chest. He was the strongest man I knew, and it always looked like his muscles were going to burst out of his shirt. I guess that was because he was a junk dealer and had to lift so much heavy stuff.

Uncle Shlomo was from the old country and had survived World War II, which meant he had seen terrible things. But he was the most cheerful and easygoing person in my family. All of my other aunts and uncles would tell you that it was going to rain even when the sun was shining. If they felt fine, they were sure that something would soon start hurting. But not Uncle Shlomo. Dad said that he had learned to appreciate the little joys in life.

Most important for us, Uncle Shlomo drove a truck. It was an old Canadian army truck that he had bought cheap, and it was as solid as a tank. If anything could get through the snow, that truck could.

Mom told us to get ready. We put on our boots and scarves and coats and hats and mitts and waited beside our suitcases. Marcus and Larry jostled one another to peek out the little oval window in the front door.

"There he is!" Larry cried. "I saw him first!"

"Did you see *this* first?" Marcus said, pulling Larry's hat over his eyes.

"Uncle Shlomo is driving awfully slowly," Mom said, ignoring them. "I guess even the truck is having trouble getting through all that snow. Okay, everybody, grab your suitcase. Let's go!"

When Dad opened the door we were hit with a blast of arctic air. As soon as I stepped outside, snow blew into my face. We made our way single file down the driveway. The truck growled and hiccupped by the curb. Dad heaved our suitcases into the back and covered them with a tarp. Then he and Mom squeezed in beside Uncle Shlomo while the three of us got in the back seat.

"A nice day if you're a polar bear," Uncle Shlomo chuckled. It was almost as cold inside the truck as outside, but my uncle wore only an old flannel shirt. As always, he had a toothpick in the corner of his mouth. "I got stuck three times on the way here. It was quite an adventure."

"We can't thank you enough," Mom said.

"For you, darling, anything. Me, I don't need any fancy-schmancy holiday. Give me a nice cup of tea and my easy chair to take a nap in. But people these days want more. I say fine, see Miami Beach. Now I have to concentrate on my driving."

Nobody spoke. Uncle Shlomo gripped the steering wheel as if he was trying to strangle it and peered through windshield, the wipers swishing back and forth. On either side of the road parked cars were disappearing under blankets of white. It felt like a new ice age. I half expected to see some dinosaur stumble ahead of us and collapse into extinction.

We got onto the highway, where the driving was a little better but still slow. At last Dad said, "There's the sign for the airport." Uncle Shlomo took the ramp. I rubbed the side window to see out but couldn't spot any airplanes taking off or landing. The truck slowed and then came to a halt.

"Here we are, door-to-door service," Uncle Shlomo said. "If you don't take off, call me. I'll be at home having a bowl of soup."

"But we *have* to take off," I said.

"Listen, Norman," he said in a kindly voice. "Here's a life lesson: as long as you've got your health there's nothing to complain about. But I hope you'll get your fancy-schmancy holiday. You can bring me home a souvenir."

Dad pulled out the suitcases and we fought our way through the big glass doors into the terminal. "It sure is quiet in here," Mom said. "I expected it to be crowded with people going on vacation. But I guess . . ."

My dad shook his head at her and she didn't finish her sentence. We made our way to the Air Canada check-in counter where a woman in a blue uniform with a little cap on her head was speaking into a telephone. She hung up and said, "May I help you?"

"We're supposed to be going to Miami Beach."
Dad put our tickets on the counter.

She picked them up. "We've had to cancel the last three flights. It's the same with the other airlines. Your plane came in last night. If there's a break in the weather, you might have a chance. But you'll have to wait."

"We'll wait," I said.

She put our luggage on a conveyor belt. Not only had I never been on an airplane, I'd never been to the airport. The check-in woman told us to go to gate three. We walked over to find a few other people who were also hoping to get on. My brothers and I went to the big windows and pressed our faces to the glass. There was our airplane. It was a sleek beauty, and as soon as I saw it my heart leapt with excitement.

"What kind is it, Norman?" Marcus asked.

"A DC-8," I said. "That's a real jet plane. It's got Rolls-Royce engines. It's got the most up-to-date radar technology. It can fly thirty-five thousand feet high, way above the clouds, where the air is clear and calm. If only it can get up there."

We watched as men moved around the plane, trying to keep it free of snow and ice. An announcement came on. "*Passengers of Air Canada flight 318 to Miami, we are going to begin boarding in the hope of being able to take off. Please have your tickets ready."* We were going to get on! I could hardly believe it.

"Stay together," Mom said. The five of us joined the line and made our way through a corridor to the oval-shaped opening that led to the plane. "Welcome aboard," the stewardess said, looking at our tickets. "You're all in row nineteen." We shuffled down to our seats. My parents took the two on one side of the aisle while my brothers and I had the three on the other. I wanted the window seat so I could look out, but somehow my brothers jockeyed me into the middle, where they immediately squeezed me with their elbows. I decided that I wasn't going to let anything ruin this for me. I looked around at everything—the little tray set into the seat in front of me, the overhead compartments. I wondered if this was going to be the extent of my holiday— seeing the inside of an airplane before we had to get off again.

Did we have a chance of taking off? I leaned over Marcus to look out the window and to my amazement saw that the snow had stopped falling. It even looked a little brighter out, as if the sun was trying to peek through the clouds.

"Ladies and gentlemen, this is Captain Ronald Fairbanks. It looks like we're going to get a break in the weather. The ground crew is doing a final de-icing. There's going to be a lot of turbulence in the first few minutes, so be prepared for some bumps. Nothing to worry about. Now I'll hand over the microphone to our head stewardess, who will go over the safety procedures with you."

I buckled myself in and listened to the stewardess, not because I was afraid but because I didn't want to miss a thing. Then the plane began to taxi along the runway. My brothers and I looked at one another with wide eyes. Were we really going to be flying on an airplane? Were we really going to travel over a thousand miles to get to Miami Beach? I wondered if one day in the future people would fly all the time and it would be no big deal to them, just like riding in a car. The plane picked up speed and I grabbed the armrests. There was a jolt and I could feel the wheels lift off the ground. We were in the air!

Leaning toward the window, I could see the ground receding below. The plane rattled and shook. It dropped and then became steady and dropped again.

"Are we going to be okay?" Larry asked.

"Oh sure," I said. "It's just turbulence. It'll probably get worse for a while."

"I hope not," Marcus said. "I feel kind of sick."

"Don't worry, this plane can take it. Why, we could be shaken right out of our seats and the plane would be fine. Why, we could even—"

Marcus reached forward. He grabbed the paper bag in the pocket below his tray and managed to get it open just in time to barf. Yuck! I turned away from him toward Larry. But Larry reached for his own bag and a moment later he was barfing too. All I could do was stare at the seat back in front of me. It was like listening to barfing in stereo.

The holiday had begun.

9

Just Picked

The pilot had been right; once we got over the clouds, the ride became smooth. The stewardess helped my brothers clean up and gave us a pack of Air Canada playing cards. She said that the flight was going to take just over three hours. Did any of us want to see the cockpit? My brothers weren't the slightest bit interested but I eagerly agreed.

I followed the stewardess up the aisle. She knocked

on the cockpit door and opened it. "Gentlemen," she said, "we have a visitor. His name is Norman."

The captain turned to smile at me. Then he pointed out various things among the rows of switches and dials and lights while the co-pilot beside him flew the plane. Through the windshield I had a view of the endless sky.

"Tell me, Norman," the captain said. "Do you know what kind of plane this is?"

I rattled off all the facts I knew about DC-8s. Then I told him about the balsa-wood airplanes I built. "I used to build some of those myself," the pilot said. "I think you know more than we do. George, give the young pilot one of those models."

"Roger that, Captain," said the co-pilot. He reached down beside him and pulled up a small box. I opened it as the stewardess took me back to my seat. It was a small metal replica of a DC-8 with the white and red markings of the airline. The little wheels on the undercarriage actually spun. I thought it was pretty amazing.

Fortunately, I remembered to hide it from my brothers as I sat down, slipping it into the seat beside me. The three of us played gin rummy for a while and managed not to argue too much, and then the lunch cart came up the aisle. We each got a tray with real china dishes and small silver knives and forks. Lunch was breaded chicken and green beans and little potatoes and chocolate pudding. After the trays were collected again I closed my eyes. I guess I was tired from worrying about the flight because I fell asleep.

I jolted awake when the wheels of the plane touched the tarmac. A moment later we were stopped and Dad was pulling our coats out of the overhead bins. I put mine on, slipping the model airplane into the pocket, and we began to shuffle down the aisle. Usually I let my brothers push ahead of me, but this time I got first in line.

I thanked the stewardess and then went down the portable stairway that led to the runway. Even before I was out the door I felt the heat and blinked at the brilliant light. The air was heavy with the scent of flowers. Immediately, I became too hot in my winter coat and boots. The sky above was pale blue and some strange birds with long necks flew overhead. Just past the airport building I could see a line of palm trees with their enormous drooping leaves. Palm trees!

I felt my father's hand on my shoulder. "We're definitely not in Canada anymore," he said.

We walked into the terminal building, and things looked different there too. For one thing, the men didn't wear suits like my dad was wearing. They wore short-sleeved shirts in wild colors—orange, yellow, pink. Some had patterns of flamingos or guitars on them. And they wore white trousers and white shoes. The women had on little sundresses, even ladies old enough to be my grandmother, and everyone had skin the color of copper pennies from being in the sun. It was like they were glowing.

I looked behind me to see my brothers staring just the way I was. "I feel like we're in an episode of *The Twilight Zone*," Marcus said.

We got our luggage and then piled into a taxi, Mom and the three of us squeezing into the back and Dad in front. The driver was an elderly Black man with close-cropped hair, sunglasses and gold chains around his neck. He had the air-conditioning on full blast, but Dad asked if he could turn it off so that we could open the windows.

"If you say so," the driver said. "Personally, I think air-conditioning is the greatest invention of all time."

We rolled down the windows and looked at the streets going by. Some of the palm trees had actual coconuts on them. We passed stands with signs saying

Fresh Papayas or *Just Picked Grapefruit*. We passed a white stucco house with an enormous cactus growing in front, and pots of giant flowers, like out of some science fiction movie.

"It's so colorful," Mom said. "It makes everything at home look so drab."

"Mr. Driver?" Larry said.

"Uh-huh?"

"Is everyone here rich?"

"Sure we are. In fact, I just drive this cab for a hobby."

"Oh."

"I'm just kidding. And you're on vacation. All you have to do is enjoy yourselves. Can I give you a little piece of advice?"

"Please do," Dad said.

"Don't lie in the sun too much on the first day, or you'll get a sunburn so bad you won't be able to sit down. Happens all the time."

"Thank you," Mom said. "We'll be careful."

We drove for another few minutes and then we began to pass big hotels, one after another. Between them I caught glimpses of the beach and the ocean. My heart beat faster.

"Which one is ours?" I asked.

"The Royal Palm is just ahead."

And there it was, a pink castle rising as if in a fairy tale. The rows of windows glinted in the sun and a line of flags on the roof fluttered in the breeze. The driver slowed down and pulled into the long entrance, stopping under the giant overhang. A man in a uniform with gold braid on the shoulders came forward to open the doors.

"Welcome to the Royal Palm Hotel," said the doorman. "I'll take care of your luggage. You go right in."

The five of us stayed close together as we passed through the high glass doors into the lobby. A dozen pink columns rose to a domed roof painted with a copy of Michelangelo's Sistine Chapel ceiling, which I recognized from one of Mom's art books. The floor was black marble and there were giant vases everywhere, brimming with jungle-sized flowers. Just like at the airport, everyone wore bright summer clothes. They carried towels, paperback novels, transistor radios, straw hats. Mom and Dad checked us in and then a porter pushing our luggage on a cart directed us to the elevators. The elevator was lined with mirrors and we looked at ourselves, five pale people in bulky winter coats and big boots, like North Pole dwellers who had taken a wrong turn.

At the thirty-fourth floor, the elevator door opened and we got out. The porter pushed the cart a little ways down the hall and then unlocked a door. "After you," he said.

Mom went in first. I heard her gasp. "This isn't a hotel room. It's a palace!"

We followed her in. She was right; it sure wasn't like any motel room we'd stayed in before. It was huge, with ceiling-high glass windows that looked down on the swimming pool and the beach. There was plush white wall-to-wall broadloom. There was a sitting room with two white sofas, and a crystal bowl of fruit on the glass coffee table. On the walls hung abstract paintings. Two doors led into the bedrooms, one for my parents and one for us. Ours had three separate beds piled with pillows, three end tables, three lamps and three dressers. We could slide open the glass door and step onto the balcony to see the ocean and feel the soft air.

"I'm never going to leave," Marcus said. "I'm going to live here forever."

"I'm going to live here for even longer," Larry said.

"You can't live longer than forever, you dope."

"Enough, you two," Mom said. "This is really

something. And we owe it all to you, Norman. But where is Dad?"

At that moment Dad came out of one of the bedrooms. He wore his bathing suit, showing off his pale, hairy legs.

"So?" Dad grinned. "Who wants to go for a swim?"

The Black Suit

I guess there are a few moments in a person's lifetime
that he's sure he'll never forget. That's what it felt like
to me, standing on the beach and looking at the ocean
for the first time.

It wasn't just blue, like I expected it to be. It wasn't
any single color. It was a whole range of blues, and blue-
green, even purple, and it got darker as it stretched out
to the horizon. And when a wave broke and rolled up
onto the beach, the water was as clear as glass.

The beach was a long, long curve of sand, as far as I could see. It looked white from farther away but was actually very pale, exactly what people meant when they said something was sandy-colored. It was warm and fine and felt good when I picked it up in my hand and let it run through my fingers, or when it slipped between my toes.

Little kids with plastic buckets picked up shells. Other kids were building sandcastles with moats that they kept filling up with seawater. Big striped umbrellas dotted the beach, with lawn chairs underneath. Fathers slept with newspapers on their faces. Mothers slathered suntan lotion on kids who were trying to get away from them. Girls in bikinis lay on their stomachs listening to transistor radios. Young guys threw footballs in the shallows.

We found an umbrella and a couple of lounge chairs for my parents, while my brothers and I set down our towels. I waited until I was really hot before running down to the water and wading in. The water was cool and lovely, and underfoot was only soft sand. I watched a wave rise toward me and held my breath as it swept me up, swirling me about before carrying me back to the beach. I came up laughing. I tasted salt on my lips.

After that I floated, or dived under, or lay in the shallows as the end of a wave washed over me. It was a while before I even noticed Marcus and Larry. They kept running into the water and throwing themselves into the oncoming wave. That looked like fun so I joined them. The three of us went under and came up again. We washed up on the beach. We chased each other and did headstands and picked up shells and I would have stayed in for a lot longer if my Mom hadn't called us out so as not to get sunburned like the taxi driver said. We came out and put on T-shirts and baseball caps and proceeded to bury Dad in the sand. Then we got out the Instamatic camera to take pictures of each of us beside him, Marcus holding up his arms to show off the big muscles he didn't have.

I didn't think it would be possible to get enough of the ocean and beach. But in the late afternoon we walked back up to the high pink wall that surrounded the back of the hotel. We went through the gate with the *Guests Only* sign to the wide deck around the swimming pool. There was a narrow bar, and waiters in black jackets bustled back and forth, carrying trays of tall, cool drinks and plates of sandwiches and bowls of ice cream. Around the outside of the deck were tables, each with an umbrella, where women and men played bridge and smoked cigars and drank glasses of beer. People were constantly jumping or diving into the pool, sending up sprays. Parents held their toddlers on the stairs, letting them splash about.

We found some lounges and Dad ordered us all sodas. When they came we lay back, sipping through straws.

"You know, Norman," Mom said. "I could get used to this. Thanks."

"You're welcome," I said. Looking around, I noticed a man who didn't seem to fit in with the scene. He was old and small and thin, with hunched shoulders. Stringy gray hair from one side of his head was plastered over the top to hide his bald spot. But what made him stand out was his suit. It was black. So were his shoes and his tie. He looked like an undertaker at a party.

He also held a miniature poodle under his arm.

The man picked up a small glass and drank it down. I said out loud, "I wonder why that man isn't wearing a bathing suit."

"Who?" Dad asked, opening his eyes. He squinted toward the bar. "Holy smokes. Is that really him?"

"Who?"

"Why, I thought he was dead. I thought he died a long time ago. He must be really, really old. But that's him. That's Mort Ziff."

"Mort Ziff?"

"You've never heard of him? I guess you're too young. Mort Ziff was a famous comedian. He played all the big nightclubs. He had his own radio show, back before there was television. And then when television came, he used to be a guest on *The Milton Berle Show*. I remember that he moved out here—they used to call him the Mayor of Miami Beach. But I haven't heard about him in years."

"Was he funny?" I asked.

"I thought so at the time. He had this peculiar style. He would make a joke, pause, make another joke, pause again. Never smiled. The jokes had nothing to do with one another. But times change. He'd probably be considered old-fashioned now. I suppose he's retired. You're seeing a real celebrity, Norman, comic royalty. That's pretty neat."

I stared at Mort Ziff and his little dog. He didn't look like a comedian. He didn't look funny at all. I took a sip of my soda and when I looked up again he was gone.

"Cannonball!" Marcus shouted, rising from his lounge and hurling himself at the pool.

"You shouldn't run," Mom said without looking up from her magazine.

"You're right, Mom," Larry said. Then he shouted, "Belly flop!" and ran after Marcus.

I got up and walked to the pool, slipping from the stairs into the warm water. An elderly woman wearing a rubber bathing cap floated by on an air mattress. A little kid rode on his dad's shoulders. I held my breath and slipped under. Opening my eyes, I saw legs waving around me. When I spotted my brothers I swam toward them and came up again.

"I have a good idea," Marcus said. "Let's all hold our breath underwater until one of us passes out."

"I don't think that's possible," I said.

Marcus just made a face and went down. Larry pinched his nose and followed. All I could do was go under too, although I had no intention of passing out. Underwater, Marcus's hair floated like seaweed. With his cheeks puffed with air, he looked like a squirrel. Larry waggled his ears. I turned around and let myself sway in the deliciously warm water, listening to the strange muffled sounds, like in a dream. It felt weirdly peaceful.

And then suddenly three other faces appeared. Three faces with dark waving hair like seaweed floating around their oval swim masks.

Marcus, Larry and I bobbed up, gasping for air. A moment later the three faces came up too. Three hands pushed back the masks to reveal three girls. They looked like sisters, about the same ages as us.

The oldest girl said, "This is our pool."

"What do you mean 'our'?" Marcus asked.

"We got here before you," said the middle one. "We got here yesterday."

"Yeah?" Larry said. "Well, you're ugly."

"And you're stupid."

"You better stay out of our way," said the oldest girl. "Or else."

"Or else what?" asked Marcus.

"You don't want to find out."

"Yeah," said the middle one. "We're from New Jersey."

The oldest one looked at her sisters and put on her mask. The others did the same and then they sank under the water and were gone. Only the youngest hadn't said anything.

"Who are they?" Larry asked.

"I don't know," Marcus growled, "but those girls don't know who they're messing with."

Horvath, Horvath and Horvath

Even on holiday, parents could be completely illogical. My mother insisted that we all take showers before dinner, even though we'd just spent about four hours submerged in water.

And then, to make matters worse, she made us put on our matching blazers, clip-on ties, beige pants and brown leather shoes.

"The dining room is very fancy-schmancy, as your uncle Shlomo would say. They won't let you in without a jacket and tie. But you all look so handsome."

"I look handsome," Marcus said. "They look like nerds."

"It'll be worth it," Dad said. "The food is supposed to be great."

Personally, I didn't see how you could enjoy eating if you were choking to death from a buttoned-up shirt. Mom put on her favorite earrings and then we filed out of the room and waited for the elevator. When it opened, I was surprised to see the girls from the swimming pool with their parents. They wore pale blue dresses and looked as uncomfortable as we were. The adults said hello and the father of the girls asked if this was our first night.

"You're going to love the food," the other dad said. "The portions are huge. Yesterday I had a steak bigger than the plate it was on."

"We're the Horvaths," said the mom. "These are our girls, Gloria, Danielle and Amy."

"How nice," Mom said. "And these are our boys, Marcus, Larry and Norman."

The elevator doors opened and we all piled out. Gloria, the oldest girl, and Marcus hissed at each other.

The Royal Palm Dining Room was the biggest restaurant I had ever seen. It was like a glittering cave, everything dark except for the chandeliers sparkling overhead. The tables all had white cloths and vases of roses on them.

"I can see those Horvath girls across the room," Marcus whispered to us. "Horvath, Horvath and Horvath. Do they ever look stupid in those dresses."

"They might be saying the same thing about us," I ventured.

When our dinners came, the portions were as enormous as Mr. Horvath had said. My brothers and I had all ordered spaghetti. "These meatballs are as big as my head!" Marcus said happily.

"The one on the right kind of looks like you," Larry said seriously.

"It does. Look, I'm going to eat my own face!"

Just then the chandeliers dimmed. A spotlight lit up a microphone stand and a stool on a small stage at the end of the room. The recorded sound of an orchestra began and then a voice boomed over hidden speakers.

"*Ladies and gentlemen! The Royal Palm Dining Room is proud to present a legend in his own time. He's the king of comics, the maestro of merriment, the sultan of sarcasm. Please welcome the unofficial mayor of Miami Beach . . . Mort Ziff!*"

Everyone in the dining room looked at the

microphone. Into the spotlight shuffled the man I had seen at the pool. He wore the same black suit and, just as at the pool, he held his little dog.

"Look at that guy!" Marcus laughed. "He's got a comb-over. What a schmo."

"Ssh," I hissed. "He's comic royalty."

Mort Ziff went up to the microphone. He looked out at the audience without smiling.

"What an ugly crowd. The last time I saw a crowd this ugly was at my family reunion."

People laughed. Mort Ziff still didn't smile. He leaned toward the mic.

"The first time I came into this place I said, 'Waiter, do you serve crabs here?' He said, 'We serve anyone. Sit down.'"

"I went to my doctor and said, 'Doctor, my hair is starting to fall out. Can you give me something to

keep it in?' He said, 'Well, I have an old shoebox.'"

"Maybe you're surprised to see me with a dog. Actually, she's a guard dog. In fact, the other day a gang of hoodlums surrounded me and asked for all my money. This dog saved my life. She used her sharp teeth to pull the wallet out of my pocket and give it to the hoodlums."

"You know, I wasn't always a comedian. In fact, I once had a job in a store. But I had to leave it because of illness. My boss got sick of me."

"Do you know who's the owner of this magnificent hotel? Herbert Spitzer. That's right, the reclusive millionaire. Herbert Spitzer sees nobody, not even me. But I'll tell you how he got so rich—by counting his pennies. In fact, the other day he was out for a walk when he saw a little boy crying. He asked, 'Why are you crying?' The little boy answered, 'Because I had two quarters and a bigger boy came by and took one of them.' Herbert Spitzer said, 'Did you call out for help?' and the little boy said, 'Just like this' and demonstrated. The millionaire said, 'Is that as loud as you can shout?' 'Yes it is,' said the boy. So Herbert Spitzer took his other quarter."

Mort Ziff went on for half an hour, making one joke after another. Dad leaned over to me and said, "I remember that he used to be funnier." But I thought he was funny. It wasn't just what he said, it was the way he never smiled or raised his voice. Even at the end when we applauded he looked sour, like he'd just eaten a lemon. Then he shuffled off the way he had come on.

For dessert I had a giant wedge of cheesecake covered with strawberry sauce. Finished at last, we all struggled to get up.

"I ate enough for three," Dad said.

"Me too," Larry agreed. "And I can't wait to do it again tomorrow."

As it turned out, the Horvaths got up at the same time as us. Our parents talked about how full they were. Behind them walked the six of us, me and my brothers on one side and the sisters on the other.

"So tell me," Marcus said, "are you up for a challenge?"

"What sort of challenge?" asked Gloria.

Marcus tried not to grin. "Ping-Pong. In the games room tomorrow after breakfast. I'll play any of you. Unless you're too scared."

"Don't make me laugh," said Gloria. "I'll play you."

"What are you kids talking about back there?" asked Mrs. Horvath.

"Oh, we're just making plans to play Ping-Pong," sang Gloria in an innocent voice.

"Aren't holidays wonderful for making friends?" said Mom.

We rode up in the elevator together. The Horvaths were a floor above us, so we got out first. As I stepped

out I looked back and saw the youngest sister—
Amy—looking at me.

She winked.

Our first day in Miami Beach seemed a week long.
I lay in my luxurious bed with its fluffy pillows and
satiny sheets and listened to my brothers sleeping in
their own beds. Marcus made a sort of hiccup sound,
while Larry was a nose whistler. I didn't mind; I was
used to them. I wondered if I made a noise when
I slept too. Maybe like a donkey or a lawn mower
starting. I remembered the joke that Mort Ziff made
about the kid and the quarter and it made me laugh
again. And I thought of Herbert Spitzer, owner of
the Royal Palm Hotel. Somebody in the lobby had
said that the floor of his penthouse was studded with
jewels and that he ate on silver plates.

Now I was feeling drowsy. I wondered why Amy
Horvath had winked at me. Probably it was a trick.
She was trying to lure me into a trap. That was my
last thought as I drifted off to sleep.

The Quest 3000

I awoke to the chatter of birds, strange sounds that I'd never heard before. My brothers were still asleep so I got up and went to the big, open windows. There were wisps of cloud in the sky. The day was already getting warm. I could smell the ocean. Was it really freezing back home, with snowdrifts piled high? I could hardly believe it. Winter already seemed far away.

Marcus and Larry got up and stood beside me in their pajamas. We looked at the long, deserted beach and the waves coming in. I waited for them to notice how amazing the weather was here.

Marcus said, "Gloria Horvath is going to wish she'd never played Ping-Pong in her life."

The ground floor of the hotel was divided into two halves, with the lobby in the middle. On one side was the dining room and also some meeting rooms and ballrooms for weddings and stuff like that. On the other side was everything else—gift shop, hair salon, the games room and a coffee shop.

As well as a Ping-Pong table, the games room had a row of pinball machines that you didn't have to pay to use, a foosball table and three shelves of board games. As we walked in there were only a couple of younger kids playing pinball. Marcus immediately took a ruler out of his pocket and began measuring the Ping-Pong net to make sure it was regulation height. Then he sprinkled talcum powder on his hands. He took his racquet out of its case and made some practice strokes in the air. He put it down to stretch.

Gloria came in, followed by Danielle and Amy. Like us, they wore T-shirts and shorts and sneakers. Gloria was carrying her own racquet. When Marcus saw it his jaw dropped.

"Is that a Quest 2000?" he asked.

"Actually," Gloria said, "it's the new model, the 3000. So how are we going to play? One game, first to get twenty-one points?"

"That suits me fine," Marcus said. "Let's volley for serve."

A player can only win points when he's serving, and Marcus won the first serve, which made him strut around with glee. Now things got serious as the two players took their positions, feet apart, bent over, racquets at the ready. Marcus smacked the ball over the net, right on the corner, but Gloria reached back to return it. It went back and forth three times before Gloria drilled it so hard that it bounced right at Marcus and smacked him in the chest.

"Yes!" cried Danielle.

Now Gloria had the serve. She scored two easy points; Marcus was clearly rattled. Then the volleys got longer, but each time Marcus tried to nail a shot he either hit the net or went past the end of the table. Soon it was six nothing for Gloria.

But she got caught too far back when Marcus tapped the ball over the net. Now it was his turn to serve. Marcus was warmed up now and he cracked that ball over the net so fast that Gloria never had a chance. He won four points in a row just on his serve before she finally managed to hit one back. They both leapt from one side of the table to the other as the ball went back and forth. Marcus used topspin and Gloria flailed hopelessly as it went by.

"That's seven to six for me!" Marcus cried. He spun his racquet on the tip of his finger, something he had spent hours practicing back home.

"That would be useful if you were in the circus," Gloria snarled. She got ready for his serve, and this time she hit it right back, catching him by surprise. Now she was serving again.

And so it went, back and forth, with the rest of us calling out encouragement. They leapt and twirled, crouched and jumped. In Ping-Pong you have to win by two points, but now the score was tied at twenty each. Gloria got a point, then Marcus tied it up again, then he lost the serve to Gloria. Twice he was a point ahead and then hit the net. Now Gloria was one point up and only needed one more to win.

She delivered a clean serve and Marcus returned it, but he was too slow moving back toward the center of the table. Gloria beamed the ball over the net so that it hit Marcus's side of the table and bounced right over his head.

"Yes!" cried Gloria. Her sisters ran to hug her.

Larry and I went over to Marcus. I wasn't upset about losing the game; I was only worried about how Marcus was going to take it.

"You almost won." Larry patted him on the back.

But Marcus just glared across the table at the sisters.

"Those Horvaths," he hissed under his breath. "We'll get them back for this."

I wanted to say, Do we have to? But I didn't have the nerve. The three Horvath girls skipped happily out of the games room. The youngest one brushed against me as they passed and I felt a folded piece of paper pushed into my hand. I closed my fingers over it.

We took the elevator back up. Only when my brothers went into our room to change into their bathing suits did I get a chance to look at the paper in my hand. Unfolding it, I saw that it was a note written on a piece of hotel stationery.

ROYAL PALM
HOTEL

"Where Everybody Feels Like Royalty"

*Meet me in the coffee shop in
ten minutes.*

Amy

I looked sneakily around, slipped the note into
my pocket and headed for the coffee shop.

13

Grilled Cheese

The coffee shop was at the very end of the corridor and didn't even have a real name, just one of those signs on a stand with magnetic letters stuck on crookedly that said *Coffee Shop*. The wooden booths and scuffed linoleum floor and faded wallpaper made it feel like I had gone backwards in time, into one of those black-and-white movies my mother liked to watch on television. Along the walls were signed photographs of past celebrities that I didn't recognize.

One was a cowboy on a horse, playing guitar. Another was a woman in a fur coat holding up a martini glass and laughing. And then I did recognize one, a thin young man with wavy hair and a thin mustache. It was Mort Ziff. Even back then he didn't smile.

A waitress in a uniform was leaning on the counter reading the newspaper while clipping her nails. The only customers I could see were an ancient couple eating bowls of tomato soup. Should I leave? And then I saw Amy's head pop up from a booth near the back. She must have been hiding.

"Did I surprise you?" she asked as I walked over to the table.

"A little. Not as much as your note."

"I didn't want my sisters to see me talk to you. They would have called me a traitor and taken revenge."

"I know exactly what you mean."

I sat down across from her. Like her sisters, she had long dark hair with bangs over her eyes. Unlike them, she wore glasses. She said, "Okay, the reason I called you here is because I want you to hand it over."

"Hand what over?"

"The secret formula."

"The what?"

"The formula for invisibility. Come on—don't play dumb. Hand it over."

"But I don't have any formula, I swear."

Amy laughed. "I'm just kidding, Norman."

I felt myself blushing. "I knew that," I lied.

Just then the waitress came over. "If you two are finished your business deal," she said, "maybe you want to order something."

"Okay," I said. "How is the chicken pot pie?"

"We use only chickens who volunteer."

Amy said, "Did the cheese volunteer to be in the grilled cheese sandwich?"

"Do I look like somebody who talks to cheese?"

"I'd say yes," I said, wanting to get in on the joke.

The waitress smiled. "So I've got a couple of wise guys here. Just my style. My name's Deloris. How about you two big spenders share a grilled cheese sandwich and an order of fries?"

"Deal," Amy said.

We watched the waitress go back to the kitchen. "Why did you ask me here?" I said.

"Because of your brothers and my sisters. Maybe you like all this competition and rivalry and being enemies. But it drives me crazy."

"Me too," I said. "But it's hard standing up to my brothers. It's always two against one."

"Same here. But I could see you were different. So let's call it a truce between you and me and be friends."

Amy held out her hand for me to shake, but I looked at her suspiciously. "Is this a trap? Or a joke?"

"No, honest."

I reached out and we shook hands. "I'm not going to tell my brothers."

"And I'm not going to tell my sisters. But maybe we can help each other stand up to them. Don't get me wrong, I like hanging around with Gloria and Danielle. I just don't want them bossing me around all the time."

"I feel exactly the same. Okay, let's try to help each other."

Deloris came back with our order and put it between us. Amy and I discovered that we both liked vinegar on our fries. It's a fact that even a crummy grilled sandwich tastes good, and we ate happily.

"By the way," Amy said, "how are we going to pay for this?"

"My dad said if I go into a restaurant I can tell them to charge it to our room."

"So you're taking *me* out? Like on a date?"

I blushed for the second time. "I'm sorry," she laughed. "I joke too much. It's hard for me to stop."

"Me too," said a voice. The two of us looked up to see Mort Ziff standing beside our booth. His little dog was tucked under his arm. "I see you've found my favorite place," he said. "Would you mind if Napoleon and I sat with you?"

"Sure!" Amy said.

"Your dog's name is Napoleon?"

Mort Ziff put the dog beside Amy and sat next to me with a groan. "Napoleon was a little man who liked a lot of attention. The same could be said for my dog, even if she is a girl. Please, Deloris, my usual."

"A cup of hot water and dry toast coming up."

I laughed. "That's funny."

"She's not being funny," Mort Ziff said. "That really is what I always have. It's good for my digestion."

"I liked your show yesterday," Amy said.

"Me too."

"Excellent. That makes two. Nowadays people want something more up-to-date. More hip. To them, seeing me is like going to the museum to stare at the Egyptian mummy."

The waitress put down a cup and plate before him. "Thanks, Deloris. You're an angel."

"Not yet I hope."

"Did you want to be a comedian when you were a kid?" I asked.

"When I was a kid I just wanted to survive. So I made the other kids laugh. Actually, my first job was as a shoeshine boy in front of Kaminsky's Vaudeville Theater. That's where I met the gangster Toots Tochkiss. I used to bring him coffee, a donut, whatever he wanted."

Amy and I looked at each other. "You knew a real gangster?" she said.

"He was one of the nicer gangsters. He used to threaten people but he never hurt a flea. When I made him laugh he gave me a nickel. He was my first audience. Now listen, you two. You're in Miami Beach and what are you doing? Talking to a fossil. Go outside and get some fresh air. Scoot!"

"Okay, Mr. Ziff," I said. "We'll see you in the dining room tonight."

"Good," he said. "I'll try not to stink up the place."

We watched Mort Ziff go and then got up ourselves. "At last," said Deloris. "I thought I was going to have to throw you out."

But as we were leaving the coffee shop I saw my brothers coming out of the games room. "Quick,"

I hissed at Amy, pulling her behind a palm tree in a giant pot. We pressed ourselves against it until I dared to look again and see that they were gone.

"That was close." Amy let out her breath.

"Too close," I said.

White Shoes

I went up to the room, thinking that I'd never made a friend before who really understood what it was like to have two older siblings like Marcus and Larry. And there they were, sitting in front of the television watching *Planet Furball*. "Look!" Larry said when he saw me come in. "It's the episode where Captain Softpaw becomes the new head of security for rat control."

"Yeah," said Marcus. "And I'm the new head of security for *Larry* control."

The door to the room opened and our parents came in loaded down with bags and boxes. "What's that?" I asked.

"Your father and I bought some new clothes. Wait a minute and we'll try them on for you."

"Groovy, Mom," Marcus said. "We can't wait for a fashion show."

I got changed into my bathing suit, grabbed a towel and slipped on my flip-flops. *Planet Furball* was just ending and Larry turned off the TV.

"We're going down to the beach!" I called.

"Not without us to watch you in the water," Dad answered back. "Hold on another second."

The door opened and Dad came out. He held out his hands and turned in a circle for us to see his new clothes.

"Dad!" Larry wailed. "You *can't* go around like that."

"Why not? Everyone here wears clothes like these."

Dad had on a bright orange shirt decorated with rows of pineapples. His pants were white. His belt was purple. His shoes were white too. On his head was a straw hat. He looked like he might start tap-dancing.

"I think he looks adorable," Mom said as she

came out. Now we stared at her. She wore a short wrap-around skirt and a halter top.

"Ah, Mom," whined Marcus. "Your belly button is *exposed*."

"Don't be such a prude. Your father and I aren't ready for the old-age home yet. Parents can have a little fun too. Now, go on down. Don't go into the water until we get there. And wear your T-shirts and hats when you're on the beach. Remember what the taxi driver said about sunburn."

The three of us trudged to the elevator. "I can't believe those clothes," Larry said.

"What's wrong with parents?" Marcus asked. "It's like they take a holiday and immediately go insane."

Our mood changed as soon as we saw the beach. The ocean was a lighter color today, and on the distant horizon a cruise ship floated like something in a dream. We heard the putt-putt of a motor and a small airplane appeared in the air. It was pulling a banner that said *Eat at the Crab Shack.*

"What kind of plane is that, Norman?" Larry asked.

"A Cessna 140. Nice little plane."

The sun felt good on my face. We pulled off our T-shirts and flip-flops, and when I looked back I saw our parents putting down their towels. "I'm going to beat you up, ocean!" shouted Marcus. He waded into the water, and as a wave rose toward him he began to punch it with his fists as it went over his head. He came up, his hands in the air. "The new world champion, Marcus Fishbein!"

"I'm going to be champion!" Larry said, running into the water. Only my brothers, I thought, would try to box with the ocean.

Hot and tired, we headed back into the hotel. And wouldn't you know it, the Horvaths were crossing the lobby at the same time. The adults greeted each other while we kids—me and Amy included—glared. Then Amy crossed her eyes, trying to make me laugh and forcing me to look away.

"We have another challenge for you," Marcus said to the sisters. "If you aren't too chicken."

"Why should we be chicken? We already beat you at Ping-Pong," answered Gloria.

"Oh, you'll be scared all right," Larry said. "When I challenge any of you to a *Planet Furball* trivia contest."

As soon as he said the words I saw Danielle's face light up. That's when I realized that she must have been a fan of the show too. "You're on," she said. "Tomorrow in the library. Five questions each."

Suddenly Larry didn't look so confident. But before he could say anything, some sort of commotion started up near the glass doors of the hotel. We turned to see a group of teenagers jumping around and screaming.

"What's going on?" Mrs. Horvath asked.

"It looks like some celebrities are coming into the hotel," Dad said.

We stopped to watch. I could just make out a long black limousine parked in front of the doors. Then another cheer went up and the crowd parted. Four young men in thin blue suits and with mop-top haircuts entered the hotel.

"Is that . . . *the Beatles*?" Mom asked in a breathless voice.

"I don't think so," Mr. Horvath said. "But it looks a lot like them."

The teenagers followed the four young men, asking for autographs. The crowd moved past us to reach the elevators. The doors opened and the four went in. One of them leaned out and waved to the crowd. "Hello, Miami Beach!" he called in an English accent. The crowd roared as the elevator doors closed.

"Oh my gosh," said one of the girls. "I just love the Centipedes!"

The crowd melted away, leaving us and the Horvaths standing there. "Who are the Centipedes?" Mom asked.

"I think I've heard of them," Mrs. Horvath said. "They're a pop group. They imitate the Beatles. Look—"

Mrs. Horvath pointed to a sign propped on an easel beside the dining room entrance.

STARTING TONIGHT!

DIRECT FROM LONDON, ENGLAND,

THE MUSIC SENSATION . . .

THE CENTIPEDES!

"Won't that be fun!" Mom said.

"As long as I still get to eat," Larry said. "Tonight I'm having veal Parmesan."

But Amy and I looked at each other. We moved away from the others. Amy whispered into my ear, "What about Mort Ziff?"

"I don't know," I said. "He can't perform in the dining room if the Centipedes are there. This doesn't look good."

"Meet you at our spot in ten minutes." And then, because she saw her sisters and my brothers looking at us, she said in a loud voice, "And you smell bad too!"

The Grim Reaper

Upstairs, I changed quickly out of my bathing suit. Marcus started to get Larry ready for the next day's contest by asking him questions about *Planet Furball*. I told my parents that I wanted to buy a pack of gum at the gift shop and took the elevator down. When I reached the coffee shop I saw Deloris playing solitaire with an old deck of cards on the counter.

"Can I sit at a table?" I asked.

"Better than the floor," she said. "And just so you know, we're out of French champagne."

I had just sat down when Amy came in and joined me. "My dad said I could order a milkshake. Share it with me?"

"Sure."

I said, "Those four guys sure look a lot like the Beatles."

"That's the point. I guess the hotel owner thinks that they'll attract customers."

"Have you ever seen the owner? Herbert Spitzer? I've heard some weird things about him."

"I have too. I heard that his rooms are all wall-papered with hundred dollar bills. But no, I've never seen him. I don't think he ever comes down from the penthouse."

"What do you think is going to happen to Mort Ziff? I feel really bad for him."

"I know. But if the Centipedes are playing in the dining room, that must mean he's going to be out of a job. I wonder if he knows."

The waitress brought the milkshake and two straws. I tore the end of the straw wrapper and blew it at Amy—at the very same time she blew hers at me. We leaned over the tall, frosted glass and started to slurp.

"I see my young friends have become regulars."
Looking up, I saw Mort Ziff with Napoleon. "Hi,
Mr. Ziff," Amy said. "Want to join us?"

"Just for a minute. So tell me, what do you two
dangerous people want to do when you grow up."

"I want to be a chef in my own restaurant," Amy
said.

"What do you know how to cook?"

"Macaroni and cheese. Also peanut butter and
banana sandwiches."

"I would definitely dine there. And you, young
man?"

"I want to design airplanes."

"Do me a favor and design an airplane with a bed
in it so I can sleep."

I saw a man come into the coffee shop and look
around. He spotted Mort Ziff and walked toward our
table. He was skinny and wore a bow tie and didn't
smile.

"I thought I might find you here," he said,
ignoring Amy and me. "I don't know why you like
this depressing coffee shop. Mr. Spitzer is planning
to rip it out and put in a martini bar."

"There goes the neighborhood," Mort Ziff said.
"Norman and Amy, this rude man is Herbert Spitzer's

personal assistant. Or as I prefer to call him, the Grim Reaper. He's the only person allowed to be in the great man's presence. Is there something you want?"

"I don't want anything," said the man. "But Mr. Spitzer has some information he wishes me to convey to you. If you will please follow me to my desk. Right now."

Mort Ziff sighed. "When the man who writes your paycheck says jump, I always say, 'Into which hole?' Good-bye my friends, see you later."

We watched them go. "Poor Mort Ziff," said Amy. "He doesn't even know he's going to be fired. And not even by Herbert Spitzer himself but by the Grim Reaper."

I couldn't think of a word to say. At last we got up, only this time we were careful to make sure my brothers weren't in the corridor. But when we got to the lobby Amy grabbed my arm. There by the front desk were her sisters, staring right at us.

I pushed her away. "Yeah?" I said in a loud voice. "Well, you stink!"

Amy smiled at me. Then she ran to join her sisters.

Ooh-Ooh-Ooh

Once again, Mom made us take showers before dressing for dinner. I'd never been so clean in my life. And after we dressed, she lined us up—"like a firing squad," Marcus said—and combed our hair for us, telling us not to squirm.

"There," she said with satisfaction. "Don't my boys look handsome?"

Marcus immediately messed up his hair and let his tongue hang out. "Gee, thanks, Ma!" he said in a hick accent. "Ah think ah looks *real* good!"

Our reservations were for six o'clock, and we were twenty minutes early. Marcus said, "Can we look in the gift shop?"

Larry's eyes widened. "There's a gift shop?"

"Go ahead," Dad said. "Just be careful not to break anything."

We went down the corridor. Everything in the gift shop had the word *Florida* on it, along with a palm tree, a flamingo or a shark. There were scarves, ashtrays, beach balls, belts, bags, ukuleles. Larry picked up a metal penny bank made to look like a coffin. When you wound it up a little plastic skeleton arm came out to pull in the coin. On the side it said, *Greetings from Miami Beach!*

"Seeing this is the greatest part of the whole trip," Larry said.

"Better than the beach and the ocean?" I asked.

"Yup."

"Better than the swimming pool and the food in the dining room?" asked Marcus.

"Yup."

Marcus and I rarely agreed on anything, but Marcus circled his finger beside his ear to mean that Larry was crazy and I nodded. We joined my parents in the lobby, where a long line of people waiting to get into the dining room snaked around the reception desk. We had a reservation so the host took us to our table right away. So did the Horvaths, just behind us. As Amy passed by me she said, "I can't believe you put a spider down my shirt today!" Then she gave me her wink.

"Good job, Wormy!" Marcus said, slapping me on the back. But my mother gave me a disapproving look. The waiter came and I ordered the special—roast chicken and mashed potatoes. We were just having our dessert when the lights went down. Four spotlights shone on the stage and lit up a big drum kit and three guitars on stands.

Ladies and gentlemen! Direct from London! It's the pop sensation . . . the Centipedes!

The four guys we had seen in the lobby came running onto the stage. The drummer held up his sticks and banged them together as he counted, "One, two, three, four . . ." And then they started to play.

> *You are so nice, ah-ah-ah,*
> *You are so cute, ooh-ooh-ooh,*
> *And when I see you, wah-wah-wah,*
> *I feel my heart go woo-woo-woo.*

The rest of the words were drowned out by all the screaming teenagers. Suddenly they rushed toward the stage and started dancing. They shook their bodies and threw their arms in the air and looked like they had itching powder down their shirts.

"Not like the way we used to dance, that's for sure," Dad shouted over the noise.

"I think it's great!" Mom said, snapping her fingers to the beat. "Come on, Phil, let's join in."

"Mom, no!" wailed Marcus. But it was too late. Mom was already dragging Dad out of his chair.

The Centipedes played for an hour. I had to admit the music was catchy, even if the words were pretty lame. But I kept thinking about Mort Ziff, and I was sure that Amy was thinking about him too. At last the lead singer shouted, "Good night, Miami Beach!" and they rushed off the stage. We joined the crush leaving and had to wait for a free elevator to take us back to our room.

Larry turned on the television. I watched for a while and then went into the bedroom to look out the open window at the dark beach and the ocean. As I felt the soft air on my skin I wondered where Mort Ziff was.

A noise made me turn and I saw my Mom coming up beside me. "It's pretty nice here, Norman."

"Yeah."

"I just wanted to say that I know why you put a spider down that girl's shirt—Amy Horvath."

"You do?"

"It's because you have a crush on her."

"Ah, Mom—"

"I know it can be scary to talk to a girl you like. But really, Norman, it's easy. Just go up and say hi. I bet the two of you would really get along. Now, you better get ready for bed. We've got another day to look forward to tomorrow."

She kissed me on the cheek and went out again. I wanted to say something to her, but what? That I was secret friends with Amy and that if my brothers knew they would kill me? I went to put on my pajamas instead.

Cheese Asteroid

In the morning, Mom and Dad tried to convince us to go to an exercise class on the deck by the pool. "You want me to do something *healthy* on my holiday?" Marcus asked. "Next thing you'll be asking me to eat asparagus." My parents just shrugged and went by themselves.

We gave them enough time to take the elevator before leaving our room. We went to the library and sat at the table waiting for the Horvath sisters. Larry's confidence in knowing everything about *Planet Furball* seemed to have evaporated. He looked white as a sheet. Marcus started to complain about the girls being late, but then they walked in. The sisters moved silently behind us—Amy slipped a note into my hand—and then sat in the chairs on the other side of the table.

"We get to decide on the format," said Gloria. "First Danielle asks a question and Lame-Brain answers. Then they reverse. The first person to get a wrong answer loses."

"We don't care. Donkey-Breath can go first," Marcus replied.

With the insults out of the way, the game began. Danielle said, "What is the only cure for catnip poisoning?"

Larry answered right away. "Gorb oil. Now it's my turn. Which rat used a whisker to sabotage the dome's electrical grid?"

"Easy," Danielle said. "That was Bug-Eyes. How many cats were trapped in the space rover while searching for the mythical cheese asteroid?"

"Seven. Want me to name them all?"

Back and forth they went, each of them getting every answer right. It looked like neither of them could be stumped. But then Larry asked, "When a cat and a rat fell in love and ran away to the garbage zone, who betrayed them?"

Danielle froze. I could see her thinking, her eyes moving back and forth.

"Time's running out," Marcus said.

"I . . . I don't know. Was it Foulbreath?"

"It's a trick question," Larry said. "No cat and rat have ever fallen in love on *Planet Furball.*"

"Darn! I should have known."

"We won!" shouted Marcus. He and Larry leapt up and started jumping around the room. The sisters just stared glumly until they were finished and then we all filed out.

"You know," Danielle said to Larry, "a cat and a rat falling in love would be a great episode."

"Wouldn't it? But could they really survive in the garbage zone?"

"They'd have to build—"

"Hey," Marcus said. "No fraternizing with the enemy."

"That's right," said Gloria. "And now we're tied at one win each. There has to be a tie-breaking contest between those two."

She pointed at me and Amy.

"We'll think of something," Marcus said. "Right now, we're going swimming."

"We're going swimming too," Gloria said.

Marcus made a face. "It's a good thing the ocean is so big."

Alligator Ballerina

When we got back to the room, I went into the bathroom to look at Amy's note. Immediately, somebody started pounding on the door.

"Hey, Wormy!" called Marcus from the other side. "You have to beat that girl. Are you good at anything?"

Yes, I thought, I'm good at ignoring my brothers. I unfolded the note and read it.

ROYAL PALM
HOTEL

"Where Everybody Feels Like Royalty"

Our parents are making us go out after we swim. But we have to talk about Mort Ziff! Meet me at the usual, 4 p.m.

Amy

But as I came out of the bathroom, Marcus saw me shoving the note into my pocket. I froze.

"What's that?" he said. "Let me guess. Are you writing a poem? About flowers and moonlight and, oh, I don't know, what a dork you are? Let me see it."

"Maybe it's a fortune from a fortune cookie," Larry said. "I bet I know what it says. *Tonight at dinner you will be pelted with olive pits.*"

I had to think fast. "Actually, it's an algebra problem I'm trying to figure out. Want to help?"

"Oh, I would," Marcus said, "but I'm too busy doing nothing."

My father came up to us. "You won't be doing nothing for long. Listen, boys. We can't spend every day at the hotel."

"Why not?" Larry asked.

"Because there are things to see," Mom said. "The Horvaths told us they're going on an excursion, and we should too."

"You've got it all wrong, Mom," said Marcus. "We should do the *opposite* of anything the Horvaths do."

But Mom went on. "We're going to give you a choice. The first choice is an art museum."

Larry pretended to strangle himself. His face grew red and his tongue stuck out. Then his eyes rolled up and his head banged onto the coffee table.

"The second choice is an alligator ranch."

My brothers began to chant, "Alligator ranch, alligator ranch!" I thought it sounded pretty good too. We quickly got dressed and went down to catch a special tourist bus in front of the hotel. The bus drove along, stopping to let people off at a shopping mall and a golf course. Then the big hotels disappeared and we passed houses with enormous verandas and wooden swings on their porches. The houses got smaller, and then we passed rows of run-down shops and hamburger joints and fried chicken stands. After that came some scrubby grass surrounded by broken fences and then, finally, a gate with a wooden sign. *George and Martha's Alligator Ranch.*

Anyone who enjoys the thought of seeing a big man in a tiny bathing suit wrestling an alligator would have loved this place. In fact, there were alligators of all sizes—small, medium and large—including some that had just hatched out of eggs. They were about the size of a banana and we got to hold one.

At the end of our visit we went into the gift shop (Mom said that Florida had more gift shops than gas stations) where they had a lot of baby-sized plastic alligators dressed in clothes and held upright on little stands. There was an alligator dentist in a white coat holding a drill, an alligator baseball player with a bat, an alligator ballerina balanced on one foot. Only after looking carefully did I realize that they weren't made of plastic; they were *real* baby alligators that had been stuffed. Pretty creepy, I thought, but Marcus begged our parents to let him buy a stuffed alligator playing a banjo. They let him get a key chain instead.

On the bus ride back, Marcus kept pretending his key chain was a giant bee about to sting Larry's ear. So Larry took off his shoe and pretended it was a swatter. He kept waving his shoe in the air until he accidentally smacked Marcus on the chin. Marcus wrestled Larry's shoe away and threw it out the bus window. Fortunately, we were just rolling up to the front of the hotel. Larry limped around on one shoe while he looked for the other in the bushes.

It was still a warm afternoon. Larry put his shoe back on and he and Marcus said they were going up to the room to change.

"I'll be up in a minute," I told my parents. "I think I left something in the games room."

"What did you leave," Marcus asked, "your underwear?"

"No. I left my favorite . . . my favorite . . . pencil."

"You have a favorite pencil?" Larry said. "But that pencil is so dull. Get it? Dull!"

"You're the one who's going to get it," Marcus said, tweaking Larry's nose. While my parents were trying to get them to behave I scampered down the hall. I went straight to the coffee shop, where Amy was waiting in our booth.

"Sorry," I said. "We just came back from an alligator ranch."

"We were at Parrot World," Amy said. "A parrot pooped on Gloria's head."

"I can't top that," I laughed.

"Listen," Amy said. "I'm tired of being afraid of my sisters. Maybe we should try to stand up to them."

"I don't think that's a good idea—at least not with my brothers. They'll only make my life more miserable."

"You should think about it."

"Okay. But what are we going to do about Mort Ziff?"

"We should go talk to him. He must be feeling really depressed."

"Maybe he wants to be left alone."

"Then he'll tell us to buzz off. I got his room number from the front desk."

"All right, let's go."

We got up and passed by Deloris, who was folding napkins. "That's the way it is with people," she sighed. "They come and they go."

Room 313 was at the end of the hall. I knocked softly on the door, but when there was no answer Amy banged with the flat of her hand.

Mort Ziff's voice came from inside. "What's all that banging? There's a carpenter's convention, maybe?" The door opened and he stood there in his usual suit and tie. The little dog Napoleon squeezed between his feet to come up for a pat. "It's the world's youngest door-to-door salesmen," he said. "I'm afraid that I'm not buying anything today."

"Can we come in?" I asked.

He welcomed us with a flourish of his hand. His room was half the size of ours. The window looked out onto a brick wall. An open suitcase lay on the single bed.

"You're packing?" Amy asked.

"No job, no room. That's how it goes."

"It isn't fair," I said. "They can't fire you. You're the Mayor of Miami Beach. You're an institution."

Mort Ziff raised an eyebrow. "Harvard University is an institution. I'm just a guy who tells jokes."

"But where are you going to live?"

"That's the two-dollar question. My agent is trying to find me a new gig. But it seems everybody wants the young comics these days. Or else these new rock and roll bands. I've been living at this hotel for so long it feels like home. I don't know where I'll go. But listen, you shouldn't be worrying about me. You two should be out making the most of your holiday. You need to have fun. Go rob a candy store or something."

He ushered us out. We walked down the hall and took the elevator to the lobby. "I guess there's nothing we can do," Amy said.

But I was thinking. "Mort Ziff needs to perform."

"But where?"

"Here. Didn't he say this feels like his home? He needs to perform here. Just not in the dining room."

Amy looked at me with a puzzled expression. "Okay, but then where? You don't mean . . . wait a minute. Do you mean the coffee shop?"

"Exactly."

"It really is kind of a dump."

"That's why I think that the owner, Herbert Spitzer, might agree. What does he have to lose?"

"I see your point. But we'd still have to convince him. And nobody sees Herbert Spitzer. He's like— he's like the Wizard of Oz." But Amy smiled. "I guess we're just going to have to see the man behind the curtain."

"When?" I asked.

"It has to be before Mort Ziff leaves. It has to be right now."

We looked at each other, our eyes going wide. See Herbert Spitzer? See the reclusive millionaire who wears gold suits and keeps money stuffed in his refrigerator?

Amy pressed the elevator button. The doors opened.

The Penthouse

We felt the elevator rise thirty-six floors, all the way to the penthouse at the top. The elevator doors opened straight onto a reception area with white walls and a glass desk. Behind the desk sat a man in a bow tie— the same man Mort Ziff had called the Grim Reaper.

"No, absolutely not," the man said into the telephone. "Mr. Spitzer wants complete control of the company or the deal is off."

He hung up and began writing something down. I gulped as we walked up to the desk.

"Excuse me," Amy said. "We'd like to speak to Mr. Spitzer."

The man squinted at us. "Mr. Spitzer never speaks to guests. If you have a request or complaint, please go to the front desk."

"It isn't either," I said. "It's a . . . a business proposition."

He stared at me a moment and then laughed, but not as if he thought anything was funny. "Mr. Spitzer isn't interested in having a lemonade stand by the pool."

"That's all right, Myron," said a voice behind him. A door that I hadn't noticed was open and a man stood before it. He was a big man, hefty, as my dad would say, and his hair was slicked back. He didn't wear a suit made of gold, but a checked jacket and dark pants.

"And to whom do I have the pleasure of speaking?"

"I'm Norman Fishbein. And this is Amy Horvath."

"Please step into my office."

He motioned for us to come around the desk and through the door. As I went in I looked around in disbelief. His office wasn't fancy at all. It didn't have jewels in the floor. In fact, it looked like some old apartment, with a small kitchen with ancient appliances, a Formica table with matching chairs, and a snug corner with a rocking chair and an old sofa. Sitting in the rocking chair was a very old woman, peering through her glasses while she knit a sweater.

"Mama, we have guests," Herbert Spitzer said in a loud voice.

"How nice. Did you offer the young people a cold drink? I made some iced tea."

"I will, Mama."

Herbert Spitzer went over to the refrigerator. I remembered what people said—that he had a fridge full of money. But all I saw when he opened the door was milk, eggs, bread and the pitcher of iced tea. He poured two glasses.

"Thanks," I said, taking a sip.

In a louder voice Amy said, "It's very good, Mrs. Spitzer."

"I've been making it that way for fifty years."

Herbert Spitzer smiled. "You two look surprised. I've made my office match the apartment where I grew up. My mother's more comfortable that way. I hope you're having a wonderful stay at my hotel."

"Oh, we are, Mr. Spitzer," I said. "There's just one thing. Or rather, one person. Mort Ziff."

Herbert Spitzer's smile turned downward. "Mort Ziff is no longer employed by me."

"We think you've made a mistake," Amy said.

"Do you? Well, Norman, Amy, let me tell you something about the hotel business. It is very competitive. You and your families could stay at the Doral or the Hilton or a dozen others. I need to provide entertainment that people actually want. Nowadays, that means the latest, up-to-date thing. And right now that thing is the Beatles. I can't get the Beatles, but I can get the Centipedes. Did you see those crowds last night?"

"I'm sure you're right about most people, Mr. Spitzer," Amy said. "But not everybody. Our parents like Mort Ziff. We like him too. The Centipedes were fun for one night, but not for every night. We think a lot of people are going to be sorry not to see Mort Ziff perform at dinner. In fact, they might want to move to another hotel."

"Now, now," Herbert Spitzer said quickly. "Let's have none of that talk. But even if I wanted to keep Mort Ziff on, there's nowhere to put him."

"Yes, there is," I said. "There's the coffee shop."

"That dump?"

"Maybe it isn't exactly fancy. But they make a pretty good grilled cheese sandwich. If you let Mort Ziff perform there, Mr. Spitzer, then people will have a choice."

Herbert Spitzer rubbed his chin. "The coffee shop, you say? I don't see the harm in trying for a few days. We could put him on tomorrow night just to try. Of course, I couldn't pay him nearly as much. The question is whether or not he'll do it. Mort Ziff used to be a much bigger star. Playing in a coffee shop is a definite come-down."

"Maybe it isn't about the money," I said. "Mort Ziff just needs to perform."

"And anyway, it will be like a night club, won't it?" Amy asked.

Herbert Spitzer looked at us. "You two are very persuasive. Myron!" he called to the man at the desk. "Get Mort Ziff on the line."

Snort Dinko

The next day, our parents made me and my brothers take a bus tour of old Miami. "Why do we want to see anything that's old?" Larry asked, but my mother insisted that it would be fascinating. She said we would get to see a lot of buildings in the "art deco" style.

"Looks to me more like 'snort dinko' style," said Marcus, looking through the bus window. After that he kept pointing and saying, "Wow, look at that 'snort dinko' house! Look at that 'snort dinko' Laundromat!"

As soon as we got back we changed and headed for the beach. After staying there for a couple of hours, we went back to our room to change for dinner. Larry tried to convince my mother that there was such a thing as being "too clean," but she still made us take showers again. I kept trying to figure out how to convince my parents and my brothers to eat at the coffee shop tonight. My brothers loved the food in the dining room, and my parents had enjoyed dancing like teenagers to the Centipedes.

I waited until everyone was dressed in their good clothes. Dad was standing in front of the mirror, adjusting his new purple tie. He had on a yellow sports jacket. Mom was fixing the wide belt on her new dress.

There was nothing for me to do but come out with it. I tried to sound casual. "So how about tonight we, ah, eat in the coffee shop?"

"Right, Wormy," said Marcus. "And how about I give you a super-wedgie?"

"No, I mean it. I heard that Mort Ziff is performing in the coffee shop."

Dad looked at me. "Let me get this straight, Norman. You want us to eat in the coffee shop. The one that smells like boiled eggs."

"I thought you liked eggs."

"Even though all the other kids are going gaga over the Centipedes, you want to see an old comedian you'd never even heard of three days ago."

"I couldn't have said it better, Dad."

"But why? You don't laugh that much when he performs."

"That's not true. I laugh inwardly."

"Well," said Mom, "I for one am impressed. Norman isn't just like every other kid. He has his own taste."

"Yeah," Larry said. "His own *bad* taste."

"Remember, we wouldn't even be in Miami Beach if it weren't for Norman. Besides, we've seen the Centipedes two nights in a row. Unless, of course, you boys would like to dance with your mom tonight."

"Definitely not!" Marcus said.

"Okay." Dad shrugged. "Then it's the coffee shop."

Larry groaned. "Good-bye giant plate of ribs."

Marcus came up beside me and whispered into my ear. "There's something going on with you," he said. "Some secret you're not telling us. But don't worry, dear brother, I'm going to find out what it is."

He gave me a devilish smile. I gulped but didn't say anything. We headed for the elevator, and it felt a bit strange being all dressed up for the coffee shop. If my brothers had realized it, they probably would have taken off their jackets and ties, but I was glad they didn't.

Once again, we met up with the Horvaths in the elevator. Mr. Horvath looked grim. "We're not going to the dining room," he said.

"Don't tell me," Dad said. "You're going to the coffee shop instead."

"You too?" asked Mrs. Horvath.

"It's almost as if our youngest kids got together and made a plan."

"Right." Amy pretended to laugh. "As if that would ever happen."

The elevator opened onto the lobby. My brothers looked with longing at the crowd waiting to get into the dining room. "Thanks a lot, Wormy," Marcus said. "You're a real pal."

We reached the coffee shop. The sign with the crooked magnetic letters had changed. It now said—

LIVE FROM THE COFFEE SHOP!

THE COMEDY STYLINGS OF MORT ZIPP,

MAYOR OF MIAMI BEACH!

"They spelled his name wrong!" I said.

"We ran out of the letter f," said Deloris with a shrug as she came up to us. "Your usual booth, Norman? And your family in the next one, Amy?"

"You two know the waitress?" Mom sounded startled.

"She's probably just a good guesser," I said lamely.

The old couple that always ate soup was already there. Two more couples and another group of four drifted in, but that was all. The waitress dropped some menus on the table and Marcus and Larry started to grumble as soon as they read them over. We ordered fish and chips and milkshakes. When the food came we were all so hungry that even my brothers thought it tasted okay, especially with a lot of ketchup. While we ate, Deloris carried in a microphone on a stand. She put down a wooden crate for a stage.

And then Mort Ziff walked in with Napoleon

under his arm. Nobody seemed to notice him. He stared at the crate a moment and then took a careful step onto it, as if afraid it might collapse.

He tapped the microphone.

"Is this thing working?"

People looked up.

"So tell me, how's the food? I ate here about ten years ago. But I'm better now, thank you."

"I went to the shoe store today. The salesman tried to put a shoe on me. He said, 'You sure have a very large foot.' I said, 'I know, but it was the only way I could match the other one.'"

"I ran into a man I know. He said, 'You know, when my wife and I had our baby he was very cute. But as he gets older he gets a little uglier every day.' I said, 'Well, did you expect him to look like you all at once?'"

"At my age you can get a little confused. Yesterday I went into my car. I saw that thieves had broken in and stolen everything—the radio, the gearshift, even the steering wheel. Then I realized that I was sitting in the back seat."

"I met a little boy on the beach. He said, 'Do you know that in a few years astronauts will go to the moon? And after that they're going to go to the sun.' I said to the little boy, 'How can they go to the sun? It's too hot—they'll burn up.' The boy looked at me like I was a nincompoop and said, 'Well, of course they're going to go at night.'"

"You've been a very select audience. Thank you for coming. After all, I don't like to waste my time. I prefer to waste other people's time."

It was a strange thing, but being so close to Mort Ziff, watching his face, his jokes seemed funnier. Everyone laughed more. And at the end we applauded. Mort Ziff looked over at me and then at Amy. He raised one eyebrow and then the other, like a teeter-totter. He turned around and shuffled out.

A Disgrace to the Family

At the start of a holiday it feels like it will last forever, and then suddenly the end is closer than the beginning. This is what I thought on the morning of our fifth day, looking out the bedroom window.

A big pelican flapped by, juggling a fish in its mouth.

Today our parents didn't make us go anywhere. My brothers and I played our first-ever game of tennis on the hotel's tennis court. Marcus thought he was going to be instantly great at it, on account of his being good at Ping-Pong. He got pretty frustrated when the ball kept zipping out of bounds. In the end, we found it more fun to make up our own game, throwing the ball over the net and running back and forth before somebody threw it back. Then Larry accidently beamed Marcus in the head and Marcus started to chase him and that was the end of tennis.

We swam in the ocean, afterwards lying on our towels and reading old *Mad* magazines. When I opened my copy I found a note from Amy.

We both arrived at the coffee shop at the same time.

"I guess you two can't get enough of this place," Deloris said. "Must be my company."

"And the milkshakes," Amy said. We slurped on our straws while she told me about Teaneck, New Jersey, and I told her about Toronto, Ontario. I was starting to feel sorry that we didn't live in the same town.

"I thought I might find you two here."

It was Mort Ziff. Napoleon gave a bark, jumped out of his hands onto the bench and licked my chin.

"You were good last night," Amy said.

"You know, it reminded me of my early days. Sometimes there was almost nobody in the audience. But if I made one person laugh, I was happy. It's good to remember."

"And you're going on tonight?" I asked.

"I am. But there needs to be a much bigger audience or else I'm finished. So says Herbert Spitzer. Well, he does own the joint. But even if there aren't more people tonight, it was a good try. And I think I have a pretty good idea who to thank. Well, I better go and prepare for the show tonight. That basically means taking a nap. Please don't feel as if you have to come."

"Are you kidding?" I said. "We wouldn't miss it."

He smiled—almost—and left. Amy and I didn't speak as we finished our milkshakes, but I knew what we were both thinking. There just had to be a bigger audience tonight. But how could we help? If only we could get that Cessna airplane to pull a banner advertising Mort Ziff's appearance! But even if I figured out how to arrange it, we didn't have the money.

Finally, I said it out loud. "There has to be a bigger audience tonight."

"I know. And we have to help get people there."

"Exactly. But how?"

"I think I know how," Amy said. "Word of mouth."

"What's that?"

"That's when a person tells her friends about something good, and those friends tell other people, and on and on until lots of people know. We have to spread the word. I just hope there's time to do it on our own."

We heard a shout.

"There they are!"

"I told you!"

"Traitors!"

Amy and I looked up in fear. There was Marcus rushing into the coffee shop, followed by Larry, Gloria and Danielle!

Instinctively, I jumped up. So did Amy, but there was nothing we could do. They had caught us red-handed, and we were surrounded.

"Stab us in the back, will you?" Gloria said. "We should have known, Amy."

"And you, Wormy? You're a disgrace," Larry said. "To a hundred generations of Fishbeins!"

Amy looked across the table at me. I felt like I knew her so well that I could read the expression in her eyes. It was time to stand up for ourselves.

I said, "Amy and I don't want to be enemies."

"That's right." Amy nodded. "We don't want to compete with each other, either. We just want to have fun. We want to be friends."

"We are friends," I affirmed.

"Friends?" Marcus said. "Friends? Ugh! You two make me sick!"

"Me too," Gloria echoed. "And you're both going to pay for this."

"That's right," Marcus said. "You'll pay."

I took a deep breath. "Well, I don't care what you do."

"Me neither," Amy said.

Our brothers and sisters stared at us in amazement. For once they didn't know what to say.

And then Amy's eyes sort of lit up. I knew she had another idea. "What's more," she said, "we need you to stop being enemies too."

"That's right," I said. I looked at Amy. "Why do we need them to stop being enemies?"

"Because they have to help us, that's why."

I nodded and crossed my arms. "Right. You have to help us."

"Help you do what?" Gloria asked.

"Save Mort Ziff's show," I said. And then I called out, "Deloris! Bring us four more milkshakes!"

As Marcus, Larry, Gloria and Danielle sipped on their milkshakes, Amy and I explained the situation. I told them about Mort Ziff losing his job, and about how we went up to see Herbert Spitzer and got him to agree to use the coffee shop. Amy told them how he would only let Mort Ziff continue if the audience got a lot bigger, and that we had to help. She told them about word of mouth and what we had to do.

"But why should we help?" Marcus asked.

"Yeah," said Gloria. "What's in it for us?"

Amy sighed. "Does there have to be something in it for you?"

"It's better than this stupid rivalry," I said.

Marcus took a noisy slurp. "If we help, can we meet Herbert Spitzer? I've never met a millionaire. Maybe he'll really like me and decide to give me a suitcase full of money."

"I want to meet him too," Gloria said.

"Us too," added Larry and Danielle.

"Sure," I said, as if Herbert Spitzer was my best friend. "You can meet him."

"Okay, then," Marcus grinned. "Let's do it."

Amy and I told them what we needed to do. In truth, I could still hardly believe that they knew Amy and I were friends and weren't going to do anything mean to us. I guess we had given each other the courage to stand up to them. And the amazing thing was that, once they agreed, all of them got really enthusiastic about our plan. We said good-bye to Deloris and went to the lobby.

A tour group had just arrived, and everyone was standing beside their luggage, waiting to check in. We moved nearby so that they could hear us.

"Did you hear the news?" I asked in a loud voice.

"What news?" asked Amy.

My brothers said nothing. I kicked Larry in the shin.

"Ow! I mean, yes, tell us the news."

"Mort Ziff is performing tonight in the coffee shop."

"Mort Ziff?" Gloria said. "The comedian? He's so funny. He's the funniest man alive."

She said the words as stiffly as a robot. "That's right," I said. "They call him the Mayor of Miami

Beach. And he's playing the hotel coffee shop tonight. But space is limited, so you better get there early."

"I *sure* will," Danielle said.

"Me too," said Amy. "And I'll bring *all* my friends."

"You don't have any friends," Marcus said, slipping back into his usual attitude. I gave him a stern look.

He said, "I mean, I'll bring my friends too."

Amy and I walked away, then turned to see that the others were still standing there. So we had to return and get them. Then we went to the pool and repeated the act. After that we split up into pairs, me and Amy, Marcus and Gloria, Danielle and Larry. We went to the sidewalk by the side of the hotel, outside the front doors, by the hair salon inside, everywhere we could think of. Each time, we repeated our little play. Would it help? Would people believe what we said and decide to come see Mort Ziff?

When we were done, we all met back in the lobby.

"I think I got better at it," Gloria said. "I like acting. I'm going to join the drama club at school."

"All I know," Marcus said, "is that doing all this good is making me nauseous. I need to go swimming."

"That's a good idea," Amy said. "Let's all go swimming together."

"Together?" Larry said.

"You heard her," Danielle said, swatting him on the arm. "Last one to change into a bathing suit is a rotten egg!"

We ran for the elevators, at least until a bellhop told us to slow down. In the room, our parents agreed to come and watch us on the beach. We got into our suits, grabbed towels and hurried our parents out the door. When our elevator opened onto the lobby, the one next to it opened at the exact same time with the Horvaths in it. We six kids walked as fast as we could through the lobby with our parents behind us, and as soon as we touched the beach we dropped our towels, pulled off our T-shirts and shook off our sneakers and flip-flops.

"Surf's up!" shouted Gloria.

We ran across the beach and threw ourselves into the waves.

Reservations

It wasn't hard to convince my brothers to go to the coffee shop for dinner this time. And Amy's sisters felt the same way. They wanted to see if our act had worked. It was our parents who were surprised.

"Really, Marcus," Dad said. "I never would have guessed that you'd agree to go to the coffee shop a second time. I thought you loved the dining room."

"Who, me?" Marcus said. "Who needs all that food, anyway?" And then he leaned over to me and whispered, "I better get to meet that millionaire."

"Oh, sure," I whispered back, although I had no idea if Herbert Spitzer's assistant would let us in. We dressed in our good clothes and walked to the elevators. I felt awfully nervous. What if our efforts had done nothing, or had brought in just one or two more tables of people?

The elevator doors opened and we saw the Horvaths inside. "The more the merrier," said Mr. Horvath. "Are you going to the coffee shop too? I really don't know what's come over our children."

"It is a little suspicious," my mother said.

We kids all looked at each other and started to giggle. Then, when the elevator doors opened, we walked down the corridor, past the games room and the library. "Do you see what I see?" asked Amy.

I looked, shook my head, and looked again. There was a lineup waiting to get into the coffee shop. A lineup! As we got closer, I listened to what the people were saying.

"They say he's the funniest man alive."

"Mort Ziff? He's an institution! He's the Mayor of Miami Beach!"

When I turned around, Amy grinned at me. I saw Gloria give Marcus a friendly smack in the arm, and

Larry and Danielle giving each other the thumbs-up. But my father said, "I don't know if we're going to get in. That's a pretty big lineup."

Not get in? The thought had never occurred to me. But just then Deloris appeared, wearing a black dress instead of her uniform. She saw us and waved.

"There you are, Norman! We have your reservation, *Monsieur*. You too, Amy."

"Gee, thanks," Amy said, as we made our way to the booths.

"I can't take the credit. It was Mort Ziff. He said to make sure I saved you tables. And you're his guests for dinner too. Order whatever you want."

"We're Mort Ziff's guests?" Dad asked. "Norman, what's going on?"

"It's kind of hard to explain. I'll tell you later."

Deloris took our order. By now all the tables and booths were full. The lights began to dim and a new spotlight came up on the microphone. Deloris herself went up to it.

"Ladies and gentlemen, the Comedy Coffee Shop is proud to present a legend in his own time. He's the king of comics, the maestro of merriment, the sultan of sarcasm. Please welcome the unofficial Mayor of Miami Beach . . . Mort Ziff!"

Mort Ziff came through the kitchen door. As always, he had Napoleon under his arm. The room might have been crowded, but he didn't look any different. He didn't smile at all.

"What, you couldn't get into the dining room? This is what I get—a second-rate audience. Well, I promise to deliver the best second-rate jokes in town."

"At my age I go to a lot of funerals. In fact, just this morning I went to a funeral for a man named Irving Puchnik. Afterwards, I went up to his widow and I said to her, 'I don't think you'll ever find another man like your husband, Irving.' She said to me, 'So who's looking for one?'"

"Yesterday I went to the doctor. He told me that I had six months to live. But I couldn't pay his bill, so he gave me another six months."

"After my show yesterday a man came up and said that I should start teaching chemistry. I told him that I didn't know a thing about chemistry. He said, 'Well, that's as much as you know about being a comedian.'"

The crowd laughed. When he finished, Mort Ziff looked at me. He raised one eyebrow like he always did and walked out of the spotlight.

23

Everybody's Royalty

The last two days of our holiday were the best of all.

When Amy and I went to the games room we saw Marcus and Gloria in the middle of an intense Ping-Pong game.

"That's some serve you've got," Gloria said. "You'll have to show me how you do it."

"Okay, if you help me with my backhand spin."

"What's the score?" Amy asked.

"Gloria's winning thirty-two games to twenty-eight. But I'm catching up," Marcus said.

"Go on," said Gloria, "let me see that killer serve."

Amy and I smiled. When we went looking for Larry and Danielle, we found them just next door in the library. On the coffee table they had put a bunch of cardboard cutout figures and were moving them around. "Are you sure that happened in episode nineteen?" Danielle asked.

"Definitely. Speezer's rat tail accidentally hit the oxygen-release switch on the control panel."

"What are you doing?" I asked.

"We're recreating every episode of Planet Furball," Danielle said. "It's not easy to get all the details right."

"It's a very complex show," agreed Larry.

Amy and I played tennis. We swam in the pool. And of course we all had dinner in the coffee shop while listening to Mort Ziff perform. Extra tables had to be brought in, and there was standing room only at the back. People from other hotels weren't only making reservations to see the Centipedes in the dining room. They were making reservations for Mort Ziff too.

Of course we went to the beach, morning and

afternoon. Only now the six of us went together. We ran straight into the waves, which picked us up and rolled us back onto the sand. We swam, chased and splashed. We let ourselves drift in the shallows while our parents sat on the beach talking. We built not just a sandcastle but a whole system of castles, with a series of moats connecting them all. And when we got tired we sat in the sand where the end of the waves washed around us and looked out at the sky and the water.

"What's out there, anyway?" Larry asked on our last afternoon. "I mean, across the water."

It was a good question. I had no idea.

"North Africa," Danielle said.

"Really?" asked Marcus.

"I checked on a map."

I wondered what people in Africa were doing right now. Maybe I would visit some day; after all, I'd made it to Florida.

"Hey, look," Amy said, standing up. Beside her in the shallow water floated a real starfish. We all crowded around it. It really did look like a star that had fallen from the sky. I was afraid to touch it, but Larry picked it up.

He turned it over and we examined the underside, which had these openings with short hairs alongside them.

"Can we keep it as a souvenir?"

"I think it's alive," I said. "We better put it back."

"Okay," Larry said, "but first I'm going to name it. I'm going to name it Frank."

"Why Frank?" Danielle asked.

"Frank Mahovlich is my favorite hockey player."

Larry put it back and we watched as the next wave drew it out to sea.

"Good-bye, Frank," Larry said.

"Good-bye, Frank," we all repeated.

And then here it was, our day of departure. The morning felt like time was moving backwards. Instead of unpacking, we were packing. Instead of entering the room for the first time, we were leaving it for the last.

A bellboy brought down the luggage for us. We still had about an hour before we needed to go to the airport. I knew that Amy and her family weren't going until later in the afternoon so I went looking for her. There she was, talking to Deloris at the coffee shop.

"So you two are going home," Deloris said. "The place won't be the same without you. Do you think it's too early for milkshakes?"

"No!" we both said.

Now that we were going, it was hard to know what to say, so we just sipped on our straws. Back home, I thought, things might be a little different with my brothers—at least I hoped so. I had friends there, but not like Amy. Maybe she was thinking the same thing.

We thanked Deloris and walked back to the lobby, where Marcus and Gloria and Larry and Danielle immediately surrounded us.

"So?" Gloria said.

"Yeah, so?" Marcus repeated. "We want our bags of money from Herbert Spitzer."

"I know I said you could meet Herbert Spitzer. But he's a very busy man and—"

"You never even met him, did you?" Marcus said. "You just lied to get us to help you."

"We did meet him," Amy said. She looked at me. "Let's go up in the elevator. We might as well try."

"All right," I said.

We waited for the elevator doors to open, and when they did four young men in T-shirts and jeans got out.

"I hear the alligator ranch is fun," said one of them.

"Maybe they'll let you wrestle one," said another.

Only when they were past us and we were riding up in the elevator did I realize that they were the Centipedes. None of us had recognized them in ordinary clothes. And then I realized something else. They didn't sound British. They sounded American! Even their accents were fake!

We reached the penthouse and stepped into the reception area. Mr. Spitzer's assistant, Myron, was at his desk eating a banana. I thought he would be annoyed to see us, but instead he looked up and smiled.

"Oh, good. I was just going to look for you. Mr. Spitzer would like a word."

"He would?"

We followed him to the door of Herbert Spitzer's office. Myron knocked and then let us in. Just like before, his mother was sitting in her armchair. Herbert Spitzer was looking at some papers.

"Hi, Mrs. Spitzer," Amy said.

"Oh, it's the nice girl and boy again. But who are these others with you? They don't look nearly so nice."

"They're our brothers and sisters," I said.

Herbert Spitzer came toward us. "Thank you for coming," he said. "I wanted to express my appreciation for your interest in the Royal Palm Hotel. It looks like Mort Ziff is going to be here for a long time, thanks to you both."

"Our brothers and sisters helped, too," I said.

"Did they?" Herbert Spitzer said. "Very good. Well, I've decided to renovate the coffee shop just for Mort Ziff's show. We won't take away the old-fashioned charm of the place, but we'll freshen it up and add more tables. And we'll put in a proper stage. But I wanted to give you—to give all of you—something to show my gratitude."

"Okay!" said Marcus, rubbing his hands together. Mr. Spitzer went to a cupboard and took out six small boxes. He handed one to each of us. I opened the top of mine and looked in. A coffee mug. When I lifted it out I saw that it had a picture of Herbert Spitzer on it and the words *Where Everybody Feels Like Royalty!*

"Thank you," I said. "That's very nice."

"Yes, thanks," Amy said. "I can't wait to use it at home."

"Now you come back again." Mr. Spitzer wagged his finger at us. "I don't want you going to some other hotel!"

Last Look

We took the elevator down to get a last look at the beach. The pool was crowded with people, and it was weird to think that, while we were leaving, other people were just starting their holidays. Through the gate we all went. Carrying our shoes and socks in one hand and our Royal Palm mugs in the other, we walked on the warm sand.

"Hey, look!" Larry said.

I turned and saw a little dog running toward us with its tongue hanging out. Was it . . . ? Yes, it was Napoleon! She came up and stood on her hind legs, wanting to be petted.

"Good dog," I said, ruffling her ears. "Good Napoleon."

"But where's your owner?" Amy asked, crouching beside me. "Where's Mort Ziff?"

I looked around as a feeling of panic came over me. "Maybe something's happened to him," I said.

"What?" said Gloria. "You don't think . . . ?"

"He was awfully old," said Marcus. "He was always making jokes about how long he had left. I bet that's it. Mort Ziff is dead!"

"Mort Ziff dead?" I said. "*Really* dead? Just when he was starting to do well again? That's just terrible."

Amy picked up Napoleon and we stood up again. "Poor dog. You poor thing," she said soothingly. "What's going to happen to you?"

I'd never felt so sad in my life. I thought maybe I'd start crying. And just then I heard somebody call out.

"Hey! Hey, there!"

The shout came from the ocean. We all looked out and saw a head bobbing up and down in the waves.

"The water's beautiful!"

"Is that Mort Ziff?" I asked. "Swimming?"

"It is!" Danielle said.

The figure in the water began to swim toward us. And to my amazement, Mort Ziff waded out of the shallows, shaking water off himself. He might have been old and skinny and wearing a bathing suit that looked like it was made in 1901, but he was definitely alive.

"I haven't been in the ocean for twenty years," he said, shaking water out of his ears. "Can you think of anything more stupid than living in Miami Beach and not going in the water? It's so refreshing I feel young again. I'm going to swim every day from now on. I could use the exercise."

"Boy is it good to see you," I said with relief. "We thought . . . we thought . . ."

"What did you think, now?" He looked at me and his eyebrow went up. "Don't tell me! You saw the dog and thought I was dead? Really? Why, that's the last thing I'll do. Get the joke, the *last thing!*"

We all groaned. Napoleon yipped. Mort Ziff took the dog from Amy. "Thanks again, you two," he said. "And the rest of you."

"You're welcome," we said, one after another.

I watched Mort Ziff walk along the edge of the beach. Without looking back, he raised his hand to wave one last time.

🌴

When we got into the hotel we found our parents looking for us. It was time to go—a taxi was waiting with our luggage already in it.

My brothers and I hardly had time to say goodbye to the Horvath sisters. I saw Gloria give Marcus a friendly punch in the arm, while Larry and Danielle gave each other a *Planet Furball* collector card. Amy looked at me and smiled. "Maybe you'll come to Teaneck, New Jersey, some time."

"Maybe," I said, but it didn't seem likely. I wished there was something else to say, but I didn't know what.

"Come on, you three," called my father from the front doors. "We'll miss our plane."

"See you, Norman," Amy said, and then she pushed a note into my hand. "Read it on the airplane, okay?"

"Okay," I said.

Marcus, Larry and I ran to the taxi and squeezed into the backseat. The driver pulled away from the hotel and onto the road.

"Well, well," said the driver. "Look who it is."

I looked up to see the same man who had picked us up at the airport. "What a coincidence," Dad said.

I turned for a last look at the hotel. "Hey, stop shoving me," Marcus said. He reached up to flick my ear with his finger. But then he shrugged and just looked out the window.

"So, did you follow my advice?" the driver asked.

"Yes, we did," Mom answered. "And nobody got a sunburn."

"I'm glad to hear it. And you, young man," he said, gesturing to me. "Was Miami Beach everything that you hoped it would be?"

"It was," I said. "It was paradise."

The driver chuckled. "Paradise for some, true enough."

"What do you mean?" I asked.

"Oh, you don't need to worry about it."

"No, really. I want to know."

"If you say so. Did you know the great Louis Armstrong is playing trumpet in Miami Beach right now? But he's not staying in any of the fancy hotels."

"Why not?"

"Not allowed. Nor Harry Belafonte either."

"But he's my favorite singer!" said Mom. "Is there actually a law against Black people staying in Miami Beach?"

"Not anymore there isn't, but that doesn't mean it's allowed. An unwritten law, I guess. Not long ago they didn't allow Jewish people, either. Like I said, paradise for some. But I'm glad you all had fun. Now take a good look out the window. Enjoy that blue sky and those palm trees before you go home!"

On the airplane, I couldn't stop thinking about what the taxi driver had said. Everything had looked so perfect in Miami Beach, but I guess it wasn't perfect at all. I wished that I could talk about it with Amy. I remembered the note she had given me and took it out of my pocket.

ROYAL PALM
HOTEL

"Where Everybody Feels Like Royalty"

Dear Norman,

Here is my address.
22 Duckwalk Lane,
Teaneck, New Jersey, U.S.A.

You better write me!

Amy

I smiled and put the note back in my pocket. The first thing I was going to do when I got home was write.

Our lunches came and we ate them on the fold-down tables. Then my brothers and I played cards. Finally an announcement came over the speaker. *Ladies and gentlemen, this is your captain. We are beginning our descent into the Toronto airport, so please fasten your seatbelts. I'm sorry to tell you that the weather in Toronto is—cold! Freezing temperatures, and last night there was another big snowfall . . .*

I looked out the window but all I could see were a few thin clouds. Then the plane banked and I saw the ground below, an endless expanse of white crisscrossed by the darker lines of roads and highways. As we got lower and lower I could see snow piled on the roofs of houses. I could see backyard skating rinks.

The plane straightened out, went down some more, leveled and touched the runway. We rolled to a stop.

People began to get up. "Do we really have to put our winter coats back on?" Marcus asked.

"I don't want you catching cold," Mom said. "Your hats and scarves too."

The plane door opened and everyone filed up the aisle. As we got closer to the open door I could feel a chill. The stewardess smiled at us as we went through the opening onto the portable stairs that led down to the runway. The cold hit me in the face.

Inside the terminal, we pulled our suitcases from the luggage carousel. "I really wish I could have bought a stuffed alligator," Marcus said.

"Look." Dad pointed at the waiting people. "There's Uncle Shlomo!"

Sure enough, Uncle Shlomo was waiting for us just outside the doors of the terminal. He stood beside his old army truck, white puffs coming from his mouth as he breathed. We piled inside.

"So the big-shot travelers are back," he said. "Was it worth all the fuss?"

"It was lovely," Mom said.

"Very relaxing," Dad added.

"Are you kidding?" Marcus raised his voice. "Miami Beach is amazing!"

Uncle Shlomo shrugged. I looked outside. Even though it was winter the sun was shining, making the new snow sparkle. The fences and signs had little caps of snow and the bare trees were hung with glittering icicles. It wasn't hot and there wasn't an ocean but it was still beautiful.

"Let's have a snowball fight when we get home," Marcus said.

"Yeah!" came from Larry.

"Well," Dad said, "I hope you three are looking forward to the first day back to school."

Marcus moaned. "I forgot all about school."

"So?" Uncle Shlomo said. "Where is it?"

"Where is what?" Mom responded.

"The souvenir you promised me."

"Oh no! We forgot to get you something."

Uncle Shlomo laughed. "I was just kidding."

"But I have one for you," I said. I reached into the knapsack between my feet and felt for the Royal Palm Hotel coffee mug that Mr. Spitzer had given me. I passed it to Dad in the front seat, and he held it up for Uncle Shlomo to see. I didn't mind giving it up; I still had the model airplane that the pilot had given me on the flight over.

"Always the thoughtful one," my uncle said with a smile. "I'll have my coffee in it every morning and feel like I'm the big shot. Look, it's starting to snow again."

"Hey, Uncle Shlomo," I said. "You know who we saw?"

"Who?"

"Mort Ziff!"

"Mort Ziff? The comedian? I thought he was dead."

"Nope," I said. "Mort Ziff is not dead. He's very alive. In fact, I bet he's taking a swim in the ocean right now."

A Note from the Author

Back in the 1960s, when I was a kid, my family went to Miami Beach for the Christmas holiday. My playmates were my two older brothers, who (I'm glad to say) are nothing like Marcus and Larry. In those days, airline pilots often let kids visit the cockpit. In Miami gift shops you really could buy stuffed and dressed-up baby alligators. (Not anymore, thank goodness.) The Beatles really did go to Florida in 1964—there's a great photograph of them splashing around in the ocean.

And what the taxi driver tells Norman at the end? That was also true, although I didn't know it at the time.

Acknowledgments

My thanks to Rebecca Comay for reading the manuscript first, to all the kids in all the schools who heard me read from it, to Amy Tompkins for shepherding it, to Lynne Missen for making it better, and to everyone at Penguin Books.

CARY FAGAN is an award-winning author for children. His kids' books include the popular Kaspar Snit novels, the two-volume Master Melville's Medicine Show, and the picture book Mr. Zinger's Hat, winner of the Marilyn Baillie Picture Book Award and the IODE Jean Throop Award, as well as a TD Grade One Book Giveaway in Canada. He has also won the Vicky Metcalf Award for Literature for Young People and the Jewish Book Award, and been shortlisted for many children's choice awards.

Visit him at www.caryfagan.com.